# NOIR CON

★ A N D ★
OUT OF THE
GUTTER
PRESENT

# NOIR RIOT

# NOIR CON

## ★ AND ★
## OUT OF THE GUTTER
## PRESENT

# NOIR RIOT

A NOIRCON
OUT OF THE
GUTTER BOOK

# Table of Contents

# Introduction
## by Cullen Gallagher

IT'S CALLED *NOIR RIOT* because noir can't be tied down, it can't be held back, and it can't be kept quiet.

Would *Noir Calm* even make any sense?

And while there may not be any actual riots within this anthology, that's because the real riot is the product you are holding in your hand.

Noir is the riot. It always has and always will be.

Historically, noir has been a modern genre for modern times. Born out of observation and outrage, desperation and depression, noir has been the chronicle of society's darkest days. From urban alleys to middle class suburbs, and swanky penthouses to backwoods hovels, noir's geography knows no bounds. Noir penetrates everywhere. No neighborhood is safe from noir, and no person is untouched by its dark reach. The *Noir Riot* consumes us all.

The poems and stories in this anthology capture the two essences of noir: the cruel hand of fate, and the crueler hand of man. Not all mysteries are better off solved, and not all tunnels have light at their end. If we weren't already doomed from the start, our follies and fuck-ups surely would condemn us.

This anthology is a collaboration between two tireless advocates for literature's dark specter: Lou Boxer, founder of *NoirCon*, the Philadelphia-based literary convention that began in 2007 (when it was still called *GoodisCon*), and Matthew Louis, the founding editor of *Out of the Gutter* and *Gutter Books*. Both editors previously joined forces for *Atomic Noir* in 2012.

All but one of the pieces collected here were submissions that were vetted by a panel of judges comprised of authors, editors, critics, and scholars. The competition was very stiff, but the following selections represent the best and the bleakest of the bunch. The one exception is Ken Bruen. Anyone who has met Ken, even for just a minute, knows that his heart and soul are immense. When we approached him about gracing *Noir Riot* with one of his works, he told us he had something truly special: a story that was originally commissioned by the late and forever great David Thompson of Busted Flush Press, and only published in a very limited edition. David passed away in 2010 all too young at the age of 38, but his many remarkable accomplishments and unequaled passion for mysteries continue to be felt in the literary world today. David holds a very special place in many hearts, and we are blessed to be able to give a second life to this story.

Some of the writers within these pages are seasoned professionals, and some are promising up-and-comers. Whether you're reading an author for the first time or revisiting one of your favorites, we sincerely hope you enjoy *Noir Riot* and check back again for future *Gutter Books* and *NoirCon* publications.

# Trophy Hunt
## by Ken Bruen

I ALMOST HAD IT together.

Man, I came as close to havin' it sweet as it gets.

I'd like to blame Texas, just lay it all on The Lone Star, let me off the hook, throw my hands up, go

"Weren't for this goddamn state, I'd be in clover."

That's a crock.

Sure, I'm in Houston, where it's all gone down the tubes, but blame, that bird ain't gonna fly. I've been here five days and like the song goes

"Waiting on a friend."

My buddy.

My homey

My main man

We hooked up in Frisco a while back. I'd been, where else, a bar and, in a jam. The other side of serial sour Mash, things went south

Fast.

A broad was at the next table, a looker if you got past the mileage. I was in the zone, no pain, Lucinda Williams on the speakers. My disposable lighter had chucked it in, piece of shit I bought with my carton of Luckies. Guess it's why they call them disposable. Hurting my thumb, flicking that little wheel they got on there. The broad looks over ... what ... the flicking annoying her, was I like invading her space? Clocked the lines round her eyes, been round the block and before I could go

"The fuck you looking at?"

She reaches out her hand, a worn gold Zippo in her fingers, does that turn, you see it in the movies, one flip, the top open, always works. It's a tired cliché but carries an old sense of style, I dig it. I can say *dig*

1

because I was in San Francisco. I leaned over, Lucky in my mouth, she fired me up and said

"Now you're smoking."

Gave a radiant smile, her, not me, I don't do radiance, took 15 years right off her. I forget her name, one of those that ends with an I … if it was in a letter, it would have a smiley face over it. I remember she was drinking Jack, the Zippo riding on a pack of Virginia Slims. A name on the lighter, faded but still legible

"Morgan."

You gotta go … Morgan? … So I went

"Morgan?"

Her mouth turning down, she spat

"My loving husband, 24-karat bastard."

I'd met my share, asked

"He take off?"

The smile again, though dimmed, a fatigue riding her voice, said

"I wish. He's at the bar, Mr. Big, drinking his fool head off."

Things got a little confused after that. I was rubbing her knee when a pool cue blasted cross my back. The next blow would have crushed my skull, I heard a voice go

"You bushwhacking varmit."

And a body crashed to the floor, the broad screaming

"You've killed my husband."

How I met Ray, he saved my ass then and has my wing since. Small guy but built, courtesy of the State Pen. He wasn't young any more, definitely the sad end of fifty but he had some moves. We hooked up, became running buddies, took down some serious change.

Reason I was hanging in Houston.

Ray had a major score lined, ready to roll. I was a bit hazy on the details. Not my area of expertise, the planning. No, my gig was cars, guns, muscle. In two years we hadn't been rumbled, not even close. Three gigs a year, different city each time. Ray was hot on this job, said

"The Big Enchilada."

Yeah, sure.

Made me nervous right there. The joint, the graveyard is chock a block with suckers who'd resolved on the *last large heist*. But Ray hadn't picked a bum steer yet. I'd booked into The Warwick, big ol' place where a black guy opened the door, hit you with an effusiveness bordering on contempt, 24 hours in and the manners were getting on my freaking nerves.

I like to read, got the fix in the Service, did a jolt in Germany and to kill the boredom, read some McBain, got addicted, been devouring mysteries since, always got a volume in my jacket. Hit town, I hit the bookstores.

My latest fix was C. J. Box ... a game warden out in Wyoming his books were hard, violent but had a sweet sense of family like I could only dream about. Saw the photos of the dude and he always wore a Stetson, black rimmed job ... way feckin' cool ... hell, to ride the wide country, Winchester on the saddle bag, long coat like Sergio Leone's movies, I'd kill for that. Ray was scathing ... called C. J. ... the Chuckster ... fuckin' with me.

Times, not often but frequent enough, I got the feeling Ray was mocking me, not a real smart idea.

I'm not very good at waiting, get antsy, the books help. Found a mystery store in town, few blocks from the hotel.

How lucky is that?

I was searching for the new C. J., asked the manager whose face lit up, he said

"Just a moment."

And fucked off. Two dogs were wandering round the shelves and I mean yer actual canines. I dunno from breeds but they could have been King Charles, one of them kind, costs a bundle of green. Dogs like me, always have. We had a mutt when I was growing up in Omaha, my old man put a bullet in its head ... said

"Don't get too attached to nuttin."

The day I put one in his, I repeated the words.

So, I'm hunkering down, rubbing their ears and a girl appeared, mid-twenties, said

"They don't usually take to customers."

I gave her my nine-yard stare, shrug and she holds out her hand, says

"I'm McKenna."

Part of me, the mean drop, which is, I guess, most of me wanted to go

"Like I give a fuck?"

But what do you know, I liked her, she was smart, could see it in her eyes and smart ain't usually the trait I'm trawling for. I shook her hand, feeling like a horse's ass. Men and women? ... shaking hands ... wasn't meant to be, seems as awkward as it appears.

She'd one of those faces, like a kind of cheeky angel. She selected a book, handed it over, said

"You got to read this, it was nominated for an Edgar."

I want to quip

"And he's ... what? ... related to Oscar?"

Let it slide, tried to show interest, and with me, that comes 'cross as a blend of grimace and confusion

I read the author's name, Jim Hime.

The manager was back, clutching, *Trophy Hunt.*

He had a name tag, David, said

"You ever like a beer, we know a great bar."

His hand was out but I was all done with that shit, noted the name of the bar he mentioned, let his hand dangle. Got a smile from the girl.

Paid the freight and I was outta there. I'd rented a Lexus, slung the book in the back, burned some rubber. I cruised through Rice University, hating the students. They had all the advantages and it kept my rage simmering but I plastered the smile on my face. Ray had told me

"Keep a vague smile smoking, keep the marks off balance."

Where the hell was he?

Stopped at a barbecue place, endured the *Y'ALL* ... got me some vitals

Ribs

Beef

'Slaw

Couple of cold Long necks. Guy sits down opposite, puts out his hand, says

"Saw y'all in Murder by the Book, I'm Creg Hargis."

I stared at him said

"Y'all in my face is what you are pal."

Didn't faze him so I asked

"You like the heat or what?"

Been a while since the cops busted my balls but every now and then, they spot you, smell Bad 'un ... Exercise some muscle. He was tucking into a steak that was 3 inches thick, laughed, said

"Hell no, I'm an attorney."

I took a long pull of the beer, it was cold, like a woman you hurt and I sneered

"There's a difference?"

Loved it, he said

"See you bought yourself the C. J. Box, lovely man."

He was lashing into the mashed potatoes like it was his last meal, I was thinking, keep it up, might well be. He said

"Reason I sat down, figured you gonna be in town a while, you might need some legal advice."

Fuckin' with me, what lawyers do, 'cept they charge you for it, I said

"What I need is another brewski."

See how Texas he was ......

He got up, came back with two, by the neck, handed it over, said

"Here's to yah, fella."

His cell pipped, sounded like the ring tone had the new Britney tune, he answered, went

"Uh-huh ..."

Then stood, said

"Gotta run, partner. Catch you in the bar with Dave and McKenna, right?"

I had to ask

"Why'd you think I needed legal ... Ad ... vice?"

Leaned on the last, let it bleed

He was wiping the gravy from his mouth, said

"Feller like you, new in town, might be looking to rent or buy a place, wanted to save you grief. See, thing is, us mystery buffs, we're like a fraternity, help each other out. Got me a buddy, name of Jake Hiatt, you'd like him, he's a guy you'd listen to all night."

I have him the eyes I'd learned from my old man, the ones where you hope you're not in their scope, said

"'Preciate the beer, don't much buy the rest of the rap, you hear what I'm saying?"

He heard, loud and clear, and let a thin smile leak from his lips, said

"You're gonna love Texas, feel it in my water."

And he was gone.

I thought about the weapon under the dash.

A 50-Calibre Desert Eagle, heavy mother, got that custom grip, six-inch barrel. Time I was cleaning it, Ray watching, he said

"You need to get out more, buddy."

I help up the ammo, let him see it catch the light, like twisted love, said

"That there is 350-grain hollow point."

He's acted as if he didn't know me, a pause, then

"What you hunting, elephant?"

I let it slide, no biggie. Some folks, don't get firepower. I'd been reading Jason Starr back then and Ray added

"Guns and books, something out of sync there."

Blew it off. Ray tries to rile me, called me *THE GRANITE MAN* ... that occasion, I'd give him the smile he preached, he didn't like that, asked

"I say something funny?"

I let that hang a bit, let him taste it then said

"You're a smart guy, Ray, the planning and shit, no one does it better."

He waited, knew there was more and when I continued to build the smile, he snapped

"And your point is ... ?"

"You're having a pop at me, that's okay, long as you *know* I know, I'm cool with it ... But what seems odd, like ... not so smart, you're having a shot at me, a high old time, and bro, I'm holding ... an elephant stopping piece of hardware."

Could be wrong, but if I recall rightly, Ray had to work at pulling up that smile.

\*\*\*

I got back to The Warwick, the black dude on the door went

"Hope you're having a fine stay with us."

I stopped, stared at him, the goddamn heat getting to me, mosquitos been feeding off my driving arm. I said, flat tone

"Give it a fucking rest buddy."

In my room, a message from Ray, he'd be arriving noon the next day. No apology for the delay and no explanation either. Come evening, I was channel surfing, ants eating at my nerves, cabin fever. I picked up the C. J. Box, normally he'd engross me, the new one, has a hell of an opening. A slip of paper fell out, the name of the bar where the bookstore folk were headed, thought, why not?

Got lost twice trying to find it, stopped, asked for directions, got them delivered with warmth and the chorus

"Y'all."

I needed a big drink and lots of 'em.

I DON'T DO NICE … WANTED TO ROAR

"Fuck off."

Bit down.

The heat hadn't abated and the mosquitos were frenzied, fresh blood. The bar had a garden and sitting at a table were McKenna, David, and a large tough-looking hombre. They yelled

"Hey, grab a seat, have a cold one."

I did.

The waitress, gave me the mother of welcomes, asked what I'd like

"Wild Turkey, rocks, Shiner back."

You're in The Lone Star zone, go native. I'm not real big on social skills, not what you'd call a *people's person* …

Jeez, when did we learn all this weird dialogue. The big dude was Jake and he was a talker, full of stories. He nudged me at one stage, I don't take that well, he said

"Don Judson, you gotta read him."

I nodded, else I'd have bitch-slapped him.

They could sink them, I'll give them that and I was in the neighborhood, I had to reach for a word on the time, I'd near say *pleasant*. When's a guy like me gonna do pleasant? Most enjoyment for me is a hooker and a six-pack or I'm putting the Eagle in some fat fuck's face and of course, reading my mysteries. But this was like, different.

I buy a few rounds, Jake is still giving me the elbow and McKenna goes

"Come and see the safe."

What?

The booze had me mellow, I'd a buzz building and thought … sure.

Follow her into the bar, she pointed to a framed photo

"There's an Edgar winner."

I'd no reply to this, nod in what I figure to be the equivalent of *shucks*.

She showed me a solid iron gate, leading into some kind of dungeon, expected Hannibal Lecter, she said

"That was the actual vault."

I'm wondering how many times it was robbed but she's moved to the juke box, feeding it quarters, said

"You select some."

I go for Willie and Waylon, throw in some U2, show I'm cool but traditional, too. She'd chosen Van Morrison, explained

"For David."

"Madame George" kids in and she's off yakking to the waitress, I got back to the table, Jake, asked

"Like it?"

What, the vault, the song? But I'm looking at David, he's flicking through a book, in the midst of a drinking gig?

What's that all about?

Worse, looks like a children's book, he gives a sheepish grin, said *"The Spiderwick Chronicles ...* Tom DiTerlizzi and Holly Black."

Handed it to me, and I tried to act as it I gave a fuck, flip the pages, said

"Great illustrations."

And they were pretty good, couple of lines in there, like they're mocking me,

"He wished this was some kind of gimmicky vacation and not real life."

Man, culture and all that crap, what do I know, not shit from shinola but I scan those lines and figure, they're like some kind of irony, right?

Bono is wailing

"With or without you."

Jake took off for a piss and I asked David

"So you and the broad, sorry, the girl, McKenna, got something going?"

He gives me a hurt look, protests

"But ... We're friends."

I didn't get it, went

"I don't get it."

He takes a draw of his beer and I add

"What's the matter with you? She's a goddamn fox."

Jake is back, listening closely.

I realized I was giving David my street face, a little too much edge on, Jake, muscles in

"They're colleagues."

I swirled, rapped

"I ask you?"

McKenna is back, maybe sensing a little stress, smiles at me, posed

"What's your name, here we are, never got yours?"

No delay, I said

"Morgan."

Jake, fast as a ricochet

"The logo on your Zippo."

Re-assess him, maybe, to pun a bit, read him wrong. I'm settling in for a lengthy session when David said

"We better go."

Came at me outta left field, I echoed

"Go?"

McKenna is gathering her stuff, Jake also on his feet, she said

"We have a reading, Charlie Stella, tomorrow."

I'm feeling what … shit … let down, disappointed? David handed me the kid's book, said

"Enjoy."

I wanted to shout

"Goddamn children's crap, you know what you can do with that?"

I said

"Yeah, whatever."

Jake leaned over, said

"You're an interesting fellah."

I near whisper, for him only

"Pray I don't get interested in you pal."

McKenna said

"Come to the reading tomorrow."

And they're gone, what the fuck is the matter with me? I'm in a blue funk, the waitress is back, smiled

"Get you a fresh one?"

I snap

"What, you're counting?"

And she legs it. I stood, threw a mess of bills on the table, then as tip, flip the kid's book on, said

"Knock yourself out babe."

Bar of The Warwick, I had me a skinful, switched to tequila. The bar guy, with the name tag Duane, asked

"Salt … lemon?"

9

I eyeball him, said

"I look like a wetback to you."

Shut him way down.

Murderous rage in my gut, hoping some fuck would get in my face. I'm running a tab, the bar guy re-fills me in silence. Very first time that rage came out to play, I was like fourteen, a skinny kid, in Brooklyn, running point for the neighborhood wise guy. An Italian teenager, big, a riot of acne and mean, stopped me in an alley, demanded

"Turn out your pockets, ass wipe."

Last time anyone … and I mean any fucking one, tried to punk me. I carried his front teeth in my jeans for the next year. I learn then, it's not important to be strong, you only need to be fast. That Italian kid was strong, he'd needed to be to digest the teeth I didn't harvest.

The tequila continued and what is the buzz expression … *it got away from me* … yeah, it fucking galloped. Morning, came to with a pistol tapping my forehead, heard

"Freeze mother."

Opened one eye, Ray was standing over my bed, a Glock in his hand, he said

"Had you going there."

And put the gun in his belt. My head hurt, my insides like a rabid dog had chewed on them and didn't much relish the taste. Ray was wearing a gaudy shirt, snazzy pants that hurt the light and Jeez, loafers with tassels. I tried to sit. Never known Ray to carry, that was my gig. Things had changed, more than I could have imagined.

He said

"Losing your edge, partner. Time was, no one could sneak up on my point guy."

I was out of bed, rubbed my twisted gut, asked

"How'd you get in?"

He gave a hearty laugh, nothing real in it, fake leaking over the words, he asked

"What, you got amnesia? It's what I do."

Sick as I was and there's few nauseas to touch the tequila bile, I looked at him. Something was off, not just the clothes but the patter, what was that?

I stood, a spasm hit. Ray wrinkled his nose, said

"The hell you were drinking, smells like a Tijuana flop house."

I grabbed the phone, got room service, rasped

"Pot of coffee … black … couple of Advil."

Listened then shouted

"You're asking me? Get 'em in Wal-Mart but get 'em."

Slammed the phone down.

Ray, I'm not kidding here, he tut-tut-tutted. You ever heard that, it's like root canal. He said

"Testy."

I headed for the shower, Ray grabbed my arm and I stared at his hand, he let go, said

"We need to talk."

I scratched my balls, said

"Damn straight. Like maybe, the hell you been for a week. I'm sitting here, my thumb up my ass, you can't pick up the phone?"

He lowered his head, almost sheepish, said

"I was in Vegas and I got … caught."

One of Ray's failings, gambling. He'd a Jones going, reason he was over fifty and still pulling stunts. I said

"Tell me."

He ran his hand along his forehead, the fairish hair thinning, the guy was aging and not gracefully, he near whispered

"I got married."

I wanted to slug him, accused

"You've been gambling, you major cocksucker. What, blackjack, the ponies? Oh no, lemme guess, you got a major points spread?"

His hand was up, defense, expecting a blow. No one knew my hair trigger better than Ray, he's seen it up close and personal. He said

"Whoa, hold the phones buddy, bring it down a notch. You been skipping your meds, that it? It is, am I right, you swore you'd keep taking them."

I'd flushed them, goddamn pills. So okay they leveled me out, they were for, what did the shrink call them … *my episodes.*

The fuck doctors know.

Level out, flat-lining more like, so yeah, I dumped them. What was he going to do?

Shoot me.

Ray shook his head and I said

"Yeah, like you swore you'd kick the gambling."

A knock at the door, I ordered

"Get that."

Let him tip room service, last of the high rollers. I went into the bathroom, slammed the door. Checked my reflection, I did look like shit, skipped shaving, get that bad ass gig going. Had the shower cold.

It hurt.

Like fuck.

Wrapped in a towel, I came out and Ray was pouring two coffees. I sneered

"Help yourself."

A pack of Advil on the tray, I took two, dry crunched them, let that grinding sound annoy Ray as much as it annoyed my own self, took a shot of the coffee, hot, bitter strong, perfect. Ray said

"I got married."

I stared at him, said

"Thanks for the invite."

He was nervous, trying to get past it, as if we could, said

"She got me out of that jam. She's a treasure, you're gonna like her."

I did another shot of the caffeine, waiting for the jolt, I said

"I love her already."

I drained at the cup, sucking it up, loudly, sloppily, Ray, seriously irritated, continued

"Her name is Sandy."

I asked

"After a beach? Where's she from? Daytona? Lemme take a shot in the dark here, she spells it with an I?"

"What?"

"Nothing."

I pulled on a white T, had the logo … DEATH OF CAIN. Omen right there if you believe in that shaman crap. I filed it in my mind under … *caution.*

Then a pair of 501s and had to sit to pull on my boots. Ray picked up the hardback, said

"Still with the Chuckster?"

I didn't answer. He knew how to push the buttons and realizing he'd scored, he added

"Still reading this guy, huh? You think you could be a game warden, that it, buddy? Riding the hills of Montana, little wifey and gingham curtains. Got a news flash for you, Marlboro man, not even taking your meds gonna make that happen. You're a stick-up artist, and that's all you are."

The fuck.

Drunk, in Boston, our last major job, I'd outlined the vision in full detail and he'd only nodded, as if he thought it was like, do-able. Hell, I'd even bought a Stetson. Resolved now to burn the mother.

And that was the end really, with that little speech, he doomed us.

\*\*\*

Sandy was trailer trash, real bottom of the food chain. She hated me like vengeance. We took the rich guy down, the reason we'd come to Houston. I hadn't planned on Sandy being along for the ride but didn't protest. I was already in the zone, the territory of barrenness, the field of aloneness. It may be bleak but it's familiar, and it sure as shit is simple.

I had to hurt the guy, hurt him bad.

Days later, we were on the outskirts of Houston, a shitpile of cash on the back seat of the Lexus, Sandy was leaning against the fender, hooker shoes catching the glint from the sun, her plastic boobs straining against a spandex top. I had *Trophy Hunt* in my hand and Ray had the Glock in my face, said

"I'm like real sorry dude but we need the stake, gonna set us up a little business. But hey, you got your books … and … I'm letting you walk."

I sighed, flipped the book high. Ray turned, I disarmed him fast, said

"Weapons, you never paid them no mind."

Shot him twice, face and gut.

Sandy was running, the ridiculous heels catching on the asphalt, put one round in the back of her dumb head. Least now she'd something in it. I picked up the volume, dusted it off, found my mark, figured I'd another, what, hundred pages to go, wondered

"What the hell was killing them cattle in Montana?"

# Workman's Comp
## by James Campbell

I'D FINISHED CLEANING UP the kitchen at the Anxious Asp, but Arlene didn't seem taken with my idea of turning her bar into a place that served food as well as booze (with me being the cook, of course), so I was kicked back in a North Beach hustler bar contemplating what my options might be, both with regard to making my monthly nut—I was sharing a Jones Street apartment on the edge of North Beach with four other people who were more or less in the same financial boat as me, barely making it—plus, I really wanted to get enough money together to cop, so I wouldn't have to worry about just scraping by, month to month, as I had been doing for the last six months, ever since I'd returned to the City from Hermosa Beach.

When I first got back to San Francisco, I crashed at Aunt Max's for a month. I knew that I was always welcome at her place, but I never looked at my stays with her as more than way-stations on-the-way-to or on-the-way-back-from L.A., Seattle, or sometimes a short stop in Portland to see my Indian grandmother, Louise. It's funny, because four or five of my high school buddies from Seattle made these very same-type stopovers with Aunt Max in San Francisco, and they even called her "Aunt Max," although none of them were related to her, as I was. These visits from my friends and I worked out well for Aunt Max, too, as she would exact a toll from each of us during our stays—the "tolls" amounted to things like her renting a carpet-steaming/cleaning machine and having one of us clean all her carpets with it; having the grout in her shower cleaned with a toothbrush; and just in general keeping her apartment spiffy enough to serve as a backdrop for an *Architectural Digest* photo-spread.

My first week back in San Francisco, the city that I really still considered my true hometown, since my childhood had been spent there, I was hanging out in North Beach at The Anxious Asp one afternoon when the owner, Arlene, who'd I'd met a year or so before on one of my yo-yo trips up and down the coast, came in, and I told her that I needed work and asked her if she had any slots or shifts open, such as maybe relief bartender for somebody that had to be off on a certain day of the week, or any other part-time jobs of that nature. She told me that right now she could only give me maybe a shift or two a week behind the bar, but she did need the long-unused kitchen area in the room behind the bar thoroughly cleaned out. I took a quick look at the place and saw that there were easily a few weeks of 8-hour days of cleaning work there: the place hadn't been used for anything for so many years that it was filled with rat turds and dust; to really make it serviceable as a kitchen again would entail thoroughly scrubbing down every inch of that room, including the walls and ceiling. So I said, "Yeah!"

I'd been working at cleaning the kitchen for about a week. One lazy afternoon I had parts of the disassembled stove out on the sidewalk and was simultaneously engaged in a bar-top chess game with an old Italian guy who repaired stained-glass windows, a craft he told me he'd learned as a boy in Italy, when I started listening to a young guy named Peter Shea bemoan the fact that he was probably soon going to be drafted into the Army. When he happened to mention that he was sharing a nearby apartment with three other people, and that they could sure use another person to help out with the rent, I jumped right on it, saying, "I'm your person—I really don't *have* a place to stay—I've been staying with a relative of mine across town, but I really need a place here in North Beach." The chrome racks outside on the sidewalk were gradually beginning to glisten under my tutelage, I was losing the chess game, but I'd just scored a place to stay, and only a few blocks away, too. Two out of three.

Besides Peter Shea, my other three apartment co-inhabitors turned out to be Kenny and Sarah—a brother and sister act—and an art student named Caroline. Peter Shea was a native San Franciscan; a boy who'd had a strict Catholic upbringing, but who had now, by his late teens, drifted into the North Beach bohemian scene and was no longer a "believer." Kenny (who I later became good friends with and always referred to as "Pittsburgh Kenny") worked as a night watchman and manned the phones at the AAA Auto Club over in

Oakland, across the bay. Kenny, with his Fu Manchu moustache, long black hair (this was two years before The Beatles stormed the U.S. and made long hair on men fashionable); always wearing what today would be called vintage clothing, but what was then thought of by the squares as just thrift-store or hand-me-down items, but by hipsters or proto-hipsters like Kenny and myself as desirable "finds," in the same way that we would appreciate discovering any pre-shoddy-mass-production-age still-utilizable well-made and/or artistically-designed thing, as part of our conscious rejection of the Madison Avenue-created Middle America Fantasy World that our senses were constantly bombarded with by all the communications media that, by the end of the 1950s, were telling us what the perfect woman was wearing, the perfect man was drinking and smoking, and what perfect car the perfect family was driving to their perfect vacation. Kenny was an avid reader as well, and his particular method of choosing apparel was quite interesting to me: he would deck himself out in items of clothing that he imagined the authors he was reading at the time would have worn. For example, I'd run into him at The Asp or wherever, and always say something like, "Oh, Kenny, I see you've got your checkered Kerouac shirt on this evening." I could see by his amused expression that he realized that I was "in on the joke," and that my confirmation of his literary apparel had hit the mark, and he always seemed to get a kick out of my usually correct guesses as to who he was supposed to "be." The subject matter of his reading mania was quite catholic, too, and his AAA night-shift job had landed him in the perfect place to indulge his passion. At this particular juncture, the French existentialists had just been translated into English for the first time, and were being published in paperback editions cheap enough for anybody who was interested to be able to afford to read them, and a lot of people *were* interested.

Back when I'd lived in Hermosa Beach, a neighbor of mine who was an East Coast Jew-boy trust-fund-baby, and was attending Chouinard Art Institute at the time, was the first person I met who was well read enough to be familiar with writers all the way from Dostoyevsky to Camus, Sartre, and the other Existentialists. During one of our talks about art and artists, and how visual artists and writers usually played off of each other's works to mirror their cultural times, I'd mentioned to him that I was trying to make my way through *The Idiot*, and dug the story and what I thought was the author's point of view to a certain degree, but the prose didn't come alive for me because it was so flat. At that time, I never even considered that I was reading what later would be characterized by almost all critics as a very badly executed translation. I'd been turned off to reading novels at all for the past couple of years because, in high school, I'd read *The Catcher in the Rye*, and then Salinger's Glass family stories, as well as Ayn Rand's *Atlas Shrugged*, along with other bestsellers such as *The Man in the Gray Flannel Suit*— these were touted as being the books to read in the late 1950s; the ones that supposedly spoke to "my" generation— but I felt no kinship with any of these writers or any of their characters or ideas. I thought Holden Caulfield was a jerk, and I knew for a fact that none of them were speaking *to* or *for* Lucky Paola! I'd been so unimpressed, in fact, that I'd lost interest in even looking for anything to read that might be in tune with my particular sensibilities, or reflective of the world that I had personally experienced. When I mentioned my difficulties in getting into *The Idiot*, my art student buddy said, "Forget about that for a while ... I'll be right back," as he left the room. He returned and handed me a copy of *The Stranger*, saying, "Read this and let me know what you think."

This first novel by Camus started me reading more of his work, as well as that of Sartre and other "existential" writers, so I shared the enthusiasm for them that Pittsburgh Kenny exhibited through the apparel that he chose to wear.

Anyway, I was sitting there in a hustler bar on the edge of the financial district, close to Clown Alley, the famous burger joint, wondering how in the hell, now that the kitchen clean-up was done and Arlene could only give me a couple shifts a week behind the bar at the Asp—not really enough even to live on, let alone build a stash of cash to use as cop money—I could put together any kind of a roll at all, certainly not enough to get back to what I really *wanted* to be doing, which was dealing kilos of weed. Kenny Cohen—not the "Pittsburgh Kenny" that I shared the apartment with—breezed into the bar while I was contemplating my financial fate. He was well known in the underworld of San Francisco as a creative box man—as opposed to a "pete man," who'd actually blow a safe *up*, a "box man" would either "peel" or drill and punch a safe to gain entry. I'd talked to him several times before, and had related to him stories of my tutorage in the Art of B&E by Hillbilly Norm down in Hermosa Beach. Kenny Cohen had been amused when I'd told him that Norm claimed that there'd never been a building put up that he could not get into. I'd noticed that Kenny always wore a suit, but to my way of thinking, he had the body type that would never look "right" in an off-the-rack suit—he should have had all of his clothes custom-tailored, and I certainly hope that he finally climbed up on enough money to have a tailor make his clothes, because otherwise, given his barrel-shaped torso combined with his Ashkenazy Jew's permanent five o'clock shadow, topped off with the black, horn-rimmed Buddy Holly glasses he always favored, well … you get the picture. He actually would have looked more natural wearing a turban with flowing Beduin robes.

Anyway, I motioned Kenny over to where I was sitting and he angled his trajectory over to my table, pulled out a chair, and sat down. As he was approaching, the infamous "Kenny Cohen smile" had appeared on his face; the smile that was usually reserved for either big-titted blondes or marks. Since I was in neither of those categories, I immediately asked him: "What just put you on Happy Street?"

"*You*, man!" was his studiedly hipsterish reply.

"Me!?!? I know you don't need to blow any smoke up my ass, man, so what's up?"

"No I really mean it … you!"

"Kenny … you'll have to break it down to me. What's so great about seeing *me* moping around in a dark bar in the middle of the afternoon?"

"Man, you need a score, and so do I, and everybody knows you're the goddam planner. You can rub two goddam matches together and not just get a flame, but a whole goddam fireworks display!"

"Let's get you a drink—I need another one, anyway—and see if we can make something fly."

After Shirley set the drinks on our table and was heading back toward the bar, I looked over at Kenny, but his eyes were still glued to her sweetly rolling ass—she was a born hustler, and very desirable to all the males that came into the bar, but her old man was currently doing a bit of five to ten at Quentin for a simple porch-creeping beef. Because of the respect her old man was held in by the local underworld community, the same respect was extended to her, and nobody ever did anything out of line; just a little humorous or lighthearted flirtation. Her place in the scene was such that, if someone had made a score or was suddenly flush for any reason, they would invariably piece her off some cash to take up to her old man at Q. Her old man had had plenty of opportunities to give up his partner or a fence, but had proven to be a stand-up guy, and had taken no one along with him to prison: that was the basis of his, and her, standing in the underworld. But that was then, and the old-time Moral Code of the Underworld—if you're caught by the Law, at *anything* you don't snitch-off your partners—is, sadly, long dead, and will never return. So, all Kenny ever did was *look* at her ass, and fantasize.

After Kenny's eyes had finally given up their steatopygic quest, I said, "I've got a couple of lines in the water; so what I need to know from you is: if I can get us in, can you open a box for us?"

"James, that's what I *do*."

"Kenny ... if I research this out and come up with something that's agreeable to you, are we on? That's all I need to know, really, from you, because I'll go forward with this if I know you're on board."

"Hell, yes; I'm living on fur coats from my last job."

"Oh, the one up on—"

"Yeah. But I had to share the score with two other guys, and you know none of the regular fences would touch those coats at all—they consider them to be 'too hot,' and you know what that means—they won't give anywhere near a decent price, because they're holding that 'too hot' bullshit over your head, and they just wanta steal 'em from *us* after *we've* stolen them, the motherfuckers! I'm having to piece 'em off one at a time, so I'd like to just lay on them and do another score and sell 'em on down the road—that's the only way ever come out ahead."

"Kenny, gimme a week, and I'll come up with all the info you'll need."

"James, it never ceases to amaze me how you get all this inside information."

"Kenny, I don't feed 'em Quaaludes, then fuck 'em; I just pump 'em for information. One of the lessons I learned down in Hollywood, is that *whores know everything*. If they're speed freaks, you give 'em a little speed; if they're heroin addicts, you give 'em a little taste, buuuut—you've got to get the information *first* or they'll shine you on; you've got to hold the carrot over their heads before you give them their taste, or you'll get nothing really useful."

"Okay, then, I'll see you back here a week from today" Then I went to work, seriously.

*** 

The next day I hit the trail to follow up on some information that I already had, just to see how valid it was, and if it could be turned into a score. I was looking for Crystal (a particular one of the many "Crystals" working tricks around the City) to start with, because when I'd been bullshitting with her on Broadway a couple of weeks before, she'd told me about a trick that she'd turned at his place of business up on Divisadero. What sprang into my mind, after talking to Kenny, was that she'd said the guy had paid her right out of a safe there in his office, and I needed to verify that, to see if it would actually be worthwhile for a safe man to go in there and spend his time—we certainly wouldn't do it for, say, a few hundred dollars, if *that* was all he normally kept around the office. The hard part was going to be finding out just how much was really in that fucking safe at any given time. How much did Crystal know about this guy's setup? I had no idea. I had to know how many times she'd been with this particular trick, how often he'd paid her out of that safe—was it every time or just the once?—and how often he availed himself of her services—once a month? once a week? every other day?

The other possibility for a large score, besides the office safe, was to try to take off a ship for its payroll. Just as with Crystal's information on her office trick's safe, various whores had told me that seamen were paid in cash literally as they went onshore from Merchant Marine ships, so I knew that there would be tens-of-thousands of dollars in a ship's safe if it were hit at the proper time. But after thinking about even checking a ship burglary out with any degree of seriousness, I realized that I wasn't James Bond and that Kenny Cohen would look fucking ridiculous in a wetsuit—hell, as I said before, he looked ridiculous in a *regular* suit, what with his round Jewish face, permanent five o'clock shadow, and wearing black-rimmed Buddy Holly glasses to boot! So the ship deal was out before it'd really gotten off the ground, in my mind, at least. It was either Crystal or nothing, right now If she didn't pan out, I'd hit the bricks, talking to other whores about their tricks and their money or jewelry stashes ("Hey, baby, look what a Big Shot I am," as they flashed a bag of uncut stones, a wad of cash, or some other "impressive" shit, essentially so they wouldn't have to *think of themselves as a trick*, whereas, in a whore's eyes, stupid egotistic moves like that made them into even more of a trick: but tricks and johns never caught on to the irony of a whore's viewpoint, fortunately for me).

Crystal was sitting, center-stage, at one of the outside tables at Enrico's, and I only had to take a simple walk up Columbus, turn onto Broadway, and—BOOM!—there she was, as always, sitting in the wrought-iron chair, slightly slouched against the marble tabletop, long legs crossed in advertisement of the ecstasy that awaited her next customer—exuding meta-, if not actual physical, pheromones, way past her "personal space" and straight through the eyes and into the brains of all the passing males—the epitome of the high-class call-girl "come and get me" look. In fact, she was one of the very few working girls I knew whose presence would be tolerated without being hassled to "move on" by the owners of the various eating and drinking establishments in North Beach, or, for that matter, any other section of San Francisco. She really had "it," whatever it was!

"Hey, Crystal, I need some information—can I sit down for a minute?"

"Sure, James, any time. I've got a deal cookin' with some guys in a back booth, so I've got a while before they screw up their courage and decide what to do with me. What's goin' on?"

"Crystal, I need to know more about that trick of yours that takes you to his office up on Divisadero ... "

"Whaddaya need to know?"

"Well, last time I saw you, you mentioned something about a safe, and that he got some cash out of it to pay you. The bottom line is, I'm trying to figure out if there might be enough cash in there to take off. Can you find out, or do you know anything right now about what might be in there?"

"Well, I saw a few stacks of bills in there when he opened it up and peeled a few off one to pay me, so ... "

"Were the those stacks wrapped? What'd he take—a couple hundreds off the top ... or what ... ?"

"Yeah, he pulled a couple hundreds off a stack with a band around it just like you see in the bank."

"Whadda you think was *in* the safe? Several stacks? Just one? What?"

"I think there were three stacks, and they were all maybe four inches or so high."

"How often do you see this guy?"

"Once a week."

"When's your next date with him?"

"Tomorrow night."

"When you saw that money, and he took those hundreds off, can you remember if it was around the first? ... Or was it at the end of the month?"

"He's done it that way quite a few times, really."

"How many, exactly? ... try to remember, if you can ... "

"Oh ... I guess, at least four ... maybe half a dozen?"

"So he's done it that way at different times of the month, then?"

"Oh yeah, definitely."

"And you're seeing him tomorrow night for sure?"

"Yeah, his dates are like clockwork."

"Okay—I need you to really observe everything on your date tomorrow night; I need to know, first, what the safe looks like: Take a mental picture of it so you can draw it for me afterwards. Think about what the position of the dial is on the door; whether the hinges are showing or not showing; and any name that's inscribed on it anywhere whatsoever, even if you can only see part of it, okay? And of course, if you *can*, check out what's in the safe tomorrow night when he pays you." I gave her the old coconspirator "in-on-the-joke" smile and continued: "Remember not to let him see you or catch you having any interest in that safe, and don't act any different than usual, because if something ends up going down on this, we don't want him to have you as the first name he thinks of. Think you can do all that for me?"

"Of course, darlin'—he thinks the *world of me!*"

"This is too public, here, so let's meet up at Gino & Carlo's after your date, and you can draw the safe for me and tell me anything else that you pick up, but just *don't let him catch on that you're interested*. Okay, Doll-face, I'm outta here. It won't take very long tomorrow night, and you *know* I'll take care of you."

I met her the next night at Gino & Carlo's, and she certainly had all the goods that I'd hoped for. The name on the safe was Newcastle & Co., there were two exposed hinges on the right-hand side as you faced it, and the dial was centered, but was placed just a little bit higher than the midpoint, vertically. She also drew a picture of the safe's face—my lord! she could have been a draftsman, it was so artistically rendered and detailed. She even put little scrollwork doo-daddles on it, and I was tempted to shout out, "Enough Mama!" but I didn't have the heart to break into her concentrated artistic enjoyment, so I stayed quiet until she was done. Then I said, "Okay, Mama, did you get a glimpse of what was inside?"

"Oh, James!—this is where I really got into it. He'd pulled a couple of hundreds out, and I said, 'Oh, I have to pay some things off—can you give me this in fifties instead?' James, you're gonna love *this*: I asked him, after he gave me the fifties, if he could break one of them down into two twenties and a ten, but he said no, he didn't have anything smaller. Did I do good or what?"

"Mama, you are now nominated for the Gangster Moll of the Year Award. You *know* I'm going to take care of you on this."

"I know, I'm not worried."

"Now, when you went in, did you go in the front door or the back door?"

"We went in the front door—there's no alleyway—and, as far as I know, there is a back, but I never did really see it."

"Inside the front door, did he switch anything off?"

"No."

"Are you *sure* he didn't switch off some box you didn't see, or was there a light on, and maybe he hit something and then the light went off, or a flashing light, or anything like that at all?"

"No, I didn't see anything like that at *all*."

I left off my inquisition there, because I knew that I had to physically check out the building myself anyway, and from what I'd learned in L.A. "apprenticing" under Hillbilly Norm, the guy who claimed there'd never been a building made that he couldn't get into, I felt confident that, after I checked it out personally, I would know what kind of system or systems were being used to protect the place, and what I'd have to do to circumvent them. One of the things Norm had taught me was how to check out the main power source: for example, if there was a line running from the power source directly out to the nearest telephone pole, that meant that there was somebody on the other end of that line, working for a service, and they would snitch you off if a door, window, or one of the early motion detectors they had back then, was breached. Some of it was really laughable, because about twenty-five percent of the time, you'd start to check out a building, you'd see a security company's sticker on the door, and you'd check to see what the company had actually installed in the place, and it'd turn out that all they'd done was put a sticker on the door. I often wondered where the various building managers got those stickers—whether they bought them at the local Idiot Store, stole them outright on a visit to the security company, off their desk, or maybe actually paid a small fee to the security company for the use of their sticker—possibly *leased* the use of the fucking thing, even! I never did find out, but whatever their reasoning, it was very foolish indeed if they thought it would turn away a professional thief. I didn't consider myself to be a professional thief; in my own mind, I was a budding dope dealer, but my friendship with Hillbilly Norm in L.A. had resulted in my having obtained certain thievery skills, and in the present circumstances they might prove to be beneficial. So my next move was to check out the building myself, both for the actual location where we would enter—Norm's Axiom No. 1 was: "Locate the safest and best entryway: the entryway; just look; it's always there, the building itself will tell you: Zen and the Art of Breaking and Entering by Hillbilly Norm—and what we might have to do to circumvent whatever security they did have. There were still four or five free days before my meet with Kenny, so there was plenty of time left for me to personally check the place out.

\*\*\*

Four days later, I was sitting at the same table in the hustler bar, waiting for Kenny to march through the door. I didn't wait long; within a few minutes he appeared and walked over to the table. We exchanged our normal banter, which, as per usual among underworld hipsters, consisted of lightweight personal insults or references to recent jobs gone bad. I opened the conversation with, "By the way, how's the furrier business these days?" I probably *would* have said: "What's the frequency, Kenneth?" but that famous Dan Rather-originated absurd phrase was still a decade and a half down the road, yet to be spoken, and I'm not a time traveller, really—it only seems that way when I get to reflecting on all this.

In his best Cagney-esque side-of-the-mouth sneer, he came right back at me with, "Oh, you know how it is … it could always be better."

"Well, I think *I've* got some good news."

"Well, lay it on me—I could use it."

"Okay. I've cased the place; been out to the joint twice. As for the security, all he's got is on the doors and windows, and it all feeds into a noise alarm at the back of the building. Easy access, there. Since we're not going through either the doors or windows, we *could* just ignore it, but, just for drill, I think we oughta take it out anyway. Just to be on the safe side. It's such an easy fix, really. Our point of entry is the roof. There's a fire escape on the back that'll give us easy access up to the roof, which, by the way, they were gracious enough to position close enough to the box that I can just snip the fucker's wires on our way up and, *voilà!* no more noise alarm. On the roof it's gonna be easier than I'd even thought—there're *two* skylights up there; the only things holding them closed are three shove-latches they both just have two small hinges on the fourth side. With a glass-cutter, I can open a hole right by each latch, reach inside and, if they're not stuck, the skylight will open right up, and we can prop it open with a two-by-four. There're a bunch of two-by-fours laying right behind the building in their junk-pile, and we can take one up with us as we ascend ... I'll have some hand-tools with me, in case one of the latches is stuck or something, and if I have to, I can pry the whole fucker of there with a screwdriver. I *did* do a walk-through all the way up to the roof dressed as a service guy—gray-on-gray and gray: I was gonna have 'Butch' monogrammed on my shirt, but on second thought that seemed to be going a little too far—whadda you think?—maybe I'll actually do it before the job. I could get you a shirt, too, you know—what name wouldja want on it, anyway?"

"Well, in my fantasies about being the old air conditioning repairman who'd just happen to be invited in for lemonade by Madame in her negligée, I always wanted 'Albert,' like, you know, that guy outta Boston who used to—"

"Oh! You mean the Boston Strangler—Albert DeSalvo, I think his name was ... "

"Yeah! *That's* the guy: it'd have to be 'Albert.' But, anyway, back to reality ... "

"The other thing is, I made a guesstimation as to the height we're gonna have to drop down to the floor from that skylight, and if we take forty feet of rope with us we'll be fine. I'll go down to the marine store on the Embarcadero and take care of that." I showed him the picture that Crystal had so artistically drawn, with notes in the margin and the whole nine yards, and he responded:

"I know that safe. This'll be a piece of cake. It's a drill and punch job for sure."

"Is there anything I haven't covered that we need to know?"

"Well, what's the latest speculation on what's inside the box?"

"Crystal seems to of covered that pretty well. She's seen over a period of several times stacks of bills that're wrapped in those bank-bands, and she says that there're at least three or four stacks, and each of 'em are at least four inches tall. She even probed to the point of finding out that none of the stacks have smaller than fifties in them, by asking the trick to make change for one of the fifties he'd already given her, and he couldn't do it. She took the initiative on that one, wouldn't you say?"

"You don't think she fronted herself off, do you?"

"No—she's a *whore*; she can lie like a Major. I think we're perfectly fine from that angle."

"Can you see any difference between going on a week day or weekend?"

"No, not really: the back of the place, the way we're going up, there's no direct view from any of the surrounding buildings—they're all businesses. Off the top of my head, I'd say let's just go on with it this coming weekend—the police are busier out there with calls on the weekends and the buildings around there are empty, as far as I can tell. I went there both last Friday and Saturday to get an idea, and I didn't see any real difference between them. There weren't any lights on in any of the buildings around there on either night, so let's do it."

"Okay, that's fine with me!"

"Okay, so we've got a date for Saturday night, eh?"

"Yeah; but just keep in mind, I don't put-out on the first date."

\*\*\*

At eight o'clock sharp the following Saturday night, I pulled up in front of Kenny's apartment house on Fulton Street in the 1948 DeSoto I'd copped right before I'd returned to the City. As I mentioned before, the little old lady in Hermosa Beach—almost my next-door neighbor—had kept it pristine in her garage for years, but had finally decided to sell it because the State had determined that her eyesight was too bad to allow her to drive any more. She'd been very pissed-off when the State of California would no longer give her a driver's license, but she'd not transferred her irritation to me in selling her beloved short—a cool car was known as a "short" back in those days—and she'd given me a tremendous deal because she knew I was moving back to San Francisco "soonest" (as the Ruddy Blighters Across the Big Pond used to say), and she obviously thought I was a "nice boy," too. Maybe she was right, even, in a way. She lived just a couple of cottages down from me, a half-block off the Strand, and had actually first offered to just give me the car, but I didn't feel right about that, and the price I'd "forced" her to put on it was a pittance, in reality.

Anyway, Kenny was ready and waiting for me in front of the apartment house, and had his burglary tools rolled up in a Naugahyde "wrap-bag," such as I'd seen mechanics and even chefs carry the tools of *their* respective trade(s) around in. I drove up to Divisadero, turned left, and headed toward Pacific Heights. I drove one block past "our" building, taking a left off Divisadero, and quickly found a parking spot. Since this wouldn't be a situation like a stick-up, where you'd want your get-away car to be completely hidden so as not to come to anyone's attention either now or later, we could park in plain sight and not worry about it, as we would be silently slipping into and out of the area, presumably not drawing any heat as we did so. We got out and walked casually back toward the building, approaching from the eastern side, so we could slip into the areaway between the repository of the object(s) of our desire and the next building with the least amount of visual exposure to the street, just in case somebody happened to be looking that way at that given instant and might remember us, either then or later. As we walked between the two buildings, I commented to Kenny over my shoulder that there seemed to be nobody at all out on the streets, so everything looked cool. It was about 8:20 P.M.

As we approached the fire escape at the back of the building, I noticed a four-foot-long two-by-four laying there on the ground and said, "We'll need that … Well, I guess I'm up to bat first," and started climbing up the fire escape, pulling out the screwdriver and wire cutters I knew I'd need to render the noise alarm inoperative. Very quickly removing the two screws that held the covering plate of the alarm in place, I exposed the two wires coming from the power source that I knew I needed to clip to put it out of commission. After I'd clipped the wires, I looked back down at Kenny and said, "Okay—run silent, run deep, we're on," and started climbing on up to the roof

I'd climbed up there two times the week before, wearing my "service" uniform and carrying a clipboard, and the roof looked exactly the same now as then. A few seconds later Kenny joined me at the rear skylight. Knowing that we had three holes to make in the glass, I handed Kenny one of the two glass-cutters I'd brought along, and we both started cutting out the pieces of glass we'd need to remove to gain access to the latches, which I fervently hoped wouldn't stick and give us any trouble. Things proceeded smoothly, and all the latches slid open freely. Kenny handed me the two-by-four, and I propped the skylight open, which gave us plenty of room. I held up the plastic Macy's shopping bag that contained the nylon rope, and Kenny responded with, "Yeah, man, you gonna show me what's in your bag?"

"Kenny, you're gonna love this; it's a work of art." At the marine rigging shop, I'd had the guy custom-make our rope "ladder" so that, laid out on the ground, it looked like a "Y" with a very long tail, and attached to each of the two ends which formed the top of the "Y" was a carabiner fastener, so that when they were hooked together, we had a loop which would fit over the base of the skylight, and the long tail of the "Y" would dangle down into the room. I'd had him put knots every foot to foot-and-a-half along the dangling tail, which I assumed would give us more purchase on the rope as we climbed down and then back up.

"That *is* a work of art—it's a beauty, man."

"Here we go," and I started down the rope. I had to descend very slowly, because otherwise the rope tended to swing back and forth with me as a human pendulum, but it worked much more smoothly when Kenny came down after me, as I was holding the bottom of the rope steady for him. With both of us now in the storage room beneath the back skylight, I turned to him and said, "It's your show now, Kenny—let's do it!"

The safe was located in one of the front offices. We walked on up to the front of the building, and as we approached the safe, Kenny commented, "No surprises here; this Newcastle is just like I thought it'd be." He first tried the lever on the front, saying, "You never know, sometimes they just leave 'em unlocked with just the door closed for effect, as a fake-out. Why don't you look on the underside of all the desk drawers—sometimes they put the combination on a piece of paper taped to the underside of a drawer." As I was doing this, he started pulling the tools out of his bag. I found nothing on the bottoms of any of the desk drawers, and, just as he was setting his stuff out on the floor in front of the safe, he instructed me further with: "Why don't you look inside all those cabinet doors, up above there," indicating with a gesture the cabinets directly above the safe. None of these yielded anything of interest, however.

"Okay, brother, one last check before I start my thing: pick up the phone over there." It was an old rotary-type phone, and he said, "Sometimes they tape the number underneath the phone," but I checked and there was nothing there. "Welp, let me get to work; it's too bad we don't know the guy's birth date—let me start drilling."

While he was drilling away, I nosed around the office for maybe twenty minutes or so when all of a sudden he said, "Okay: this is the moment of truth." He had drilled two holes, one on either side of the dial. As I walked up, he picked up a punch and a small ball-peen hammer and proceeded to strike the dial with what appeared to me to be only a modicum of force, but it was enough to pop the dial back into the interior of the safe's hollow door. Two "arms" were now exposed, and Kenny proceeded to manually manipulate them to the positions that released the locking mechanism. Suddenly, he swung the door open.

We both exclaimed our respective versions of "Jesus H. Fuck!" when we caught sight of the stacks of money laying inside. What we'd come for was sitting right in front of our faces, which I'm sure were both wearing involuntary shit-eating grins from ear to ear. I quickly pulled out a laundry bag that I'd brought along to put the cash in (it was actually my Marine Corps laundry bag!) and handed it to him, saying, "Kenny, whadda you think is there?"

"Christ, man, I think it's at least double what we thought."

"Wow—you think ten grand apiece?"

"I do believe so, brother. Let's get it in this bag and get the hell out of here."

No high fives were necessary—we knew we'd *scored*. I threw all the banded stacks of money into the bag while Kenny was rewrapping his tools. We looked at each other and silently headed back to the rope. As we were going back, I said, "Kenny, you're the expert—do we leave some kind of humorous note in the safe; some great profundity for them to discover, along with no cash tomorrow?"

"Let's just get the fuck outta here!"

"Okay … *okay!*"

We got to the rope—Kenny had already strapped his tools to his body—and he put the loops from my Marine Corps laundry bag over his head and started climbing back up while I once again steadied the rope by holding it taut from the bottom during his ascent. He reached the top and climbed back out onto the roof, and out of my sight. "Okay, I'm comin' up, now."

I'd probably climbed about halfway back up the rope—maybe ten or twelve feet—when I heard a ripping sound and instantly thought of wood; I looked up and saw that the foundations of the skylight were already careening down toward me, and my next thought was, "Oh shit!—the skylight!" That was the last clear thought I had for some time.

I must have been stunned to unconsicousness for a few seconds at least, as the next thing I remember coming through my mental haze was Kenny's voice, stage-whispering, "James … James … James …"

His voice brought me back to a twilit, murky reality, but then I became aware of a tremendously painful throbbing in my left ankle. When I looked down, I saw a large piece of glass embedded in the top of my foot, just at its juncture with my ankle. *I'M FUCKED!* was my initial thought. I shouted up to Kenny, "Get the goddam money *out of here!*" But my ears were perceiving sound in the same way they would if I'd just undergone an abrupt elevation change—like all types of sounds were coming in through a barrier of water, or the kind of pressure differential you'll get sometimes while descending in an airplane—and my ears hadn't been cleared or popped yet. I was trying to talk to Kenny, but my voice seemed to me like it might be only sounding inside my own head—I couldn't tell if I was speaking with enough volume for him to hear me, so I blurted out, in what I hoped was a loud enough—but not too loud, so as to not draw outside attention—voice, "Kenny—can you *hear* me!?!?"

"Yes, yes, I hear you! I hear you!"

"Kenny, get the fuckin' money out of here, *now!*"

"What can we do to get you out of there?"

"Kenny, for the last fucking time, you go and get the money out of here!"

"Are you sure … ?"

"Yes, yes, YES!!! GO!!!"

That was my last conscious memory until I "woke up" to find myself standing back in the front office area. I looked down at my foot. The glass was gone, but as I looked around the spot where I was standing, the floor was covered with blood. I should have that wrapped, I thought, and actually spoke, sotto voce, "I gotta do this now!" as I struggled to the nearest chair, sat down, and kept repeating the mantra, "I can do this, I can do this, *I can do this …* " to keep myself awake. I took off my gray uniform shirt, which was bloodier than shit, pulled off my t-shirt, then wrapped the t-shirt around my ankle as tightly as I could, right at the wound itself, the words *direct pressure, direct pressure, direct pressure* having become the new mantra that would keep me in touch with myself and, more importantly, conscious enough to still have a shot at getting out of this fix. Yet another mantra now imposed itself over my gibbering mind: *Get the hell out of here, get the hell out of here, get the FUCK OUT OF HERE!* which finally prompted me to pick up the chair that I was sitting on and, after taking several deep breaths, hurl it with all the force I could muster straight through the front plate glass window of the building. The Venetian blinds were down, but I threw the chair with enough force that they were torn from their place of attachment on the wall over the plate glass window, and ended up draped half-over what had now become a "lower window sill," giving me the point of egress from the building that I so sorely needed. I tried to walk up to the now-open window space, but after only two "steps" I realized that my entire left leg had become an essentially useless appendage—I had no conscious muscular control over any aspect of its movement; I literally had to grab my left pant leg with my left hand and lift the leg off the floor to achieve any forward motion. At this point, I realized I'd need the help of a chair to even make it up to the window, so I looked around for a chair that wasn't fitted with fucking rollers; I spotted one, but it was much further away than I would have liked. I headed toward it anyway—I had no choice in the matter.

After I finally got the rollerless chair in hand, I used it as a "walker," and my progress back to the window was much easier, but still not really what you'd call sufficiently mobile. I knocked out a couple of spikes of glass that were still seated in the bottom groove of the window where I wanted to go through, then awkwardly pulled myself up to where I was finally sitting on the windowsill itself. Now all I had to do was somehow get off the sill and down to the sidewalk; about a four-foot drop. It was probably about 9:30 P.M., but I *still* didn't see a single soul out on the street, so I figured I could get away, if my luck held … *and I could remain conscious*!

I launched myself off the windowsill, dropped the four feet to the sidewalk, and my good right leg immediately buckled beneath my weight, causing me to fall forward onto my hands and forearms. Success!—of a sort, anyway: at least I was finally out of the fucking building.

From this point on, my awareness of what was going on around me came in short periods of "lucidity" that were really more dream-like, semi-conscious states, punctuated by long stretches of total oblivion/unconsciousness. After remaining for an indeterminate time on the sidewalk in front of the building, I next came to to find myself standing upright near the corner, with the thought swirling in my mind that I could actually go for a ways if I could *just get the right damned* rhythm *going.* My newest mantra. I'd been dragging my left leg by the pants, as before, but for some reason I felt that if I could achieve this magic rhythm, I could motate on down the road and somehow get away, just by walking. My next flash of awareness came when, somehow, I found myself now *across* Divisadero, starting to go downhill, which seemed to cause me a lot more problems than walking on a flat surface had done. I spotted a Triumph TR-3 parked just a few cars down from where I was standing and, knowing how easy it was to hotwire one of those cars, I immediately thought that it would be my ticket out of there. Then, bye-bye again, only to wake up sitting in the driver's seat. I took out my pack of Camels, saw that I'd evidently not yet tried to hotwire the car, as the foil around the cigarettes inside the pack was still intact, so my next move was to remove that foil, wad it up into a small ball the approximated the size of the three prongs that stuck out from the back of the ignition switch, smash it into that space by feel, so it was physically touching/connecting all three prongs, then push the starter button. I expected the car to start, but it did not. I fell back into unconsciousness. God knows how many times I tried to start that motherfucker, but the engine finally caught, and I thought, *Now I can really get out of here!*

I actually made it to the first intersection before I was cut off by two or three cop cars, lights flashing. I vaguely remember being lifted out of the Triumph, then I blacked out again. Later on, I found out that I'd been sitting outside that apartment building trying to start the Triumph for *almost an hour and a half* in between blackouts, and that the owners of the car had heard repeated attempts to start a car outside, had looked out their window to observe me sitting in *their* car, apparently very determined to start and steal it, and then called the police. One of the several details of that evening that remain unexplained to this day, is why it took the police an hour and a half to arrive on the scene of a car-theft-in-progress. Oh, well.

I next came to in a holding tank with a jailhouse medical orderly unwrapping my t-shirt from around my ankle. When he finished, he looked up dismayed and exclaimed, "This man has to get to the hospital immediately!" My next conscious awareness was of being in a hospital, laying on a gurney in what seemed to me to be an examination room of some type. I vaguely remember asking, several times, "Is my foot going to be all right?"

General placations were the only responses I got, such as, "Don't worry, we're going to take care of you here—we're just getting you ready for the operating room." I remember a shaving of my leg, and then a swabbing with an antiseptic, then blackness again.

I woke up the next morning handcuffed to a hospital bed in an orthopedic ward with about a dozen other patients, still a little woozy from the anesthetic, but much more clear-headed than I'd been at any time since my fall. A policeman was sitting in a chair next to my bed, watching me, but I wasn't going anywhere because, in addition to the handcuffs, my left leg was in a complete hip-cast, totally immobile, and elevated on a pulley to boot!

That afternoon I had two visitors. The first was Peter Shea, who informed me that I already had a lawyer, who was probably in court at that very moment getting me o.r.'d—released on my own recognizance—and that the policeman would be gone by the next day, and that he himself would be back after the cop had departed. The second was the young surgeon who'd operated on me. He explained to me that he'd used a fairly new technique to tie the severed tendons in my ankle back together, and that, if I followed the proper physical therapy regimen, I'd have full use of my leg and foot in the future, but it would take several months, after the cast was cut off, before I would resume normalcy in the motating department, all of which news was good to hear, because it was still sinking in that I'd almost lost my left foot and I'd probably barely skirted becoming a gimp, a fate which I'd flashed on at different points in my ordeal. I'd thought that I might end up with just a stump for a "foot," in fact, so I now gleefully realized that all the black girls I was destined to teach the finer points of buck-dancing to were still on my card.

The next day I awoke without the handcuffs or the cop present. Peter Shea showed up mid-morning to tell me both that I did have a lawyer and that he was acting as a factotum for Kenny Cohen, who didn't feel that it would be a good idea for him to visit me at this time. My lawyer was from the office of Vincent Hallaran, the famous criminal defense attorney who, along with the likes of F. Lee Bailey, Wm. Kunstler, and a very few others, was a household name throughout the United States, so I felt that Kenny Cohen had done me right. Peter asked me if there was anything I needed, and I told him to bring some reading material the next time he came up, which he did.

About a month into my stay in the hospital, a young-ish social worker turned up at my bedside one day, and asked me some general questions about my insurance status. I told her that I had no insurance at all. She then said that she'd bring up some papers for me to start filling out in that regard, and I thought no more about it at the time. Her next visit, I filled out the various forms she'd brought, and as I read through them, I realized that I was actually applying for workman's comp. When I asked her about what this meant, she said that it was simply a formal way to get the State of California to pay for my hospital bills. I was happy to go along with whatever she'd cooked up, as I knew that, what with the length of my stay and the costs of the operation, I would owe a lot of money, which I frankly didn't have. For a vocation, she had me put "agricultural salesman," after I told her that most of my money had come from selling weed in the past year. We both got a laugh out of that approach, and I thought to myself, *This young lady is going places in the world*!

About two weeks later, Peter Shea brought my mail up to the hospital, and there was a envelope from the State of California that—lo and behold!—contained a check for $460. I was amazed. Peter laid it out for me: since I'd signed up for worker's comp, they'd considered me as "injured on the job" and out of work because of that injury, and I would be paid during the period that I'd be "out of work."

"You mean, I'm going to get paid by the State of Califormia until I pull a burglary with Kenny again!?!?"

"Well … you'll get a monthly check until you're well."

And that was that. Two months after entering the hospital, I was released and went back to the Jones Street apartment on crutches, but still in a full hip-cast. All the roommates were still there but Caroline the art student, who was staying in Boston with her folks for the summer. The cast was shortened from the hip in stages, over several visits, as the doctor determined how far I'd progressed on the road to recovery, and once I'd gotten used to walking with crutches—which called upon the use of several sets of muscles I didn't know I even possessed until then—I passed my days going all over town, from Aunt Max's to the library to most my old haunts. I didn't spend any time laying around at all, and I even wore the "knob" of the bottom of my cast—this knob was a two-inch-thick, solid plaster piece that kept the cast itself from hitting the ground when I walked, which the doctor mildly chastised me for, but he couldn't argue the fact that the more exercise I got the better, to a certain extent anyway, as I was regaining the use of my leg by doing all that walking.

Since getting out of the hospital, I'd only talked to Kenny Cohen on the phone, but one day we set a time to meet down at the hustler bar where we'd originally hatched our burglary plan. When I walked in, Kenny was already there, up at the bar with a few other people that I recognized, and as I approached, a chorus of hoots, cheers, exclamations of "Right on, man!" and other comradely comments broke out A few people were even clapping.

"Kenny, what the fuck!?"

With a wider-than-usual shit-eating grin, he said, "Man, you're famous! A burglar that gets worker's comp! Completely unheard of, and *you did it!*"

I realized I'd been maneuvered into a place where I had to buy a goddam round for the house, but it hit me an instant later that Kenny probably had my share of the money from the safe with him, too, so all was well, and I didn't begrudge him his little humorous setup.

Since we had no phone at the Jones Street apartment, I was in the habit of getting my phone messages at The Anxious Asp, and there was one waiting for me to get in touch with my lawyer. I called the number and talked to a secretary, who told me that I had an appointment the very next day with my lawyer and The Man himself, Vincent Hallaran, ESQ., in his office.

The upshot of all this was that I met with the two men, and they rehearsed me to prepare for the possibility that we would have to go to trial, with Hallaran questioning me as the "prosecutor," my lawyer as my lawyer, and me as me. What it boiled down to was, I wasn't to answer any questions at all, period. He schooled me in the many ways of giving an answer without saying anything useful to the other side.

The following week was our initial court date, and I felt that I was in good hands, no matter what transpired that day. As it turned out, when we walked into court, only the judge was sitting there—the courtroom was totally empty aside from him. My lawyer walked up to the bench and said, "Your Honor, this is the case that I spoke to you about, and Judge _____ is going to hear this case in courtroom _____, and I think he's probably waiting on us right now" The judge then signed a piece of paper; handed it to my lawyer, and we walked back out into the hallway, down the corridor to the other courtroom, where another judge was indeed waiting for us. This time, there was one other person besides the judge in the courtroom; a court stenographer. A similar procedure then transpired, where my lawyer handed the piece of paper he'd gotten from the first judge to the new one, saying, "Your Honor, you'll recall that I spoke to you about this case, regarding a dismissal of all charges."

"Yes, all charges are dismissed." I noticed that the stenographer was taking all this down, and I assumed that he was officially recording the dismissal of the charges. The paper was handed back to my lawyer and we turned around and walked out. The finest justice money could buy had just been bestowed upon me. Kenny Cohen had indeed spent the greater part of my share of the score wisely. I continued to receive workman's comp checks for the next six months. They stopped coming when the hospital's physical therapist told me I didn't need to come back anymore; they'd done as much for me as they could and I was, in reality, almost walking normally by that time.

And that, my friends, is how I received workman's compensation from the State of California, in the Year of Our Lord 1962, for stealing a little more than $20,000.

# A Visit to the One-Eyed Man
## by Bill Crider

I WAS IN A CAFÉ called Mom's Place eating a bowl of chili and some crackers. Not very good chili. Too much gristle, not enough pepper. The crackers were okay, though.

Ricky Nelson was singing "Hello, Mary Lou" on the jukebox when the two men walked in and came over to my table.

Somebody once said, "Never eat at a place called Mom's." I guess he was right.

One of the men was big, about six-two, and almost as wide as the table. The other one was a lot smaller, but they were dressed just alike. Both wore dark suits, snap-brim hats, and ugly ties. The suits weren't custom made, so it was easy to see that they both wore pistols in shoulder holsters under their suit jackets.

I knew the smaller one. He was my brother, just one year younger. Same dark eyes and hair as me, except there was something missing in his eyes. Feeling, I guess. We had the same compact build, same nose, except mine had been broken and his was nice and straight. At a distance you couldn't really tell the difference, though.

"The One-Eyed Man wants to talk to you," he said.

The One-Eyed Man was Ralph Merchant, but nobody called him that. They all called him the One-Eyed Man. He didn't seem to mind. He'd lost the eye in Korea, in what they'd called a police action instead of a war. I'd missed it, myself, thanks to a bum knee that made me unfit for service.

The story was, the One-Eyed Man had been heavily involved in the black market in Korea and that he was making so much money he decided to come home. So he paid some guy to get into a bar brawl with him and gouge out his eye. I don't know if it was a true story, but

I thought it probably was. When he got back to the states, he had an eye patch and plenty of criminal contacts. He used his contacts to get into all kinds of things, none of them legal, and in only a few years he was controlling most of the crime in one end of the city.

I took a bite of chili and asked what the One-Eyed Man wanted with me.

"He'll tell you," my brother said. "Get up and let's go."

"I'm eating, Donnie," I said. "Can't he wait?"

"Don't call me that," he said. "It's Don. Now get up."

I kept sitting and took another bite of the chili.

The larger man looked around the little café. There had been only one other customer, the Ricky Nelson fan, and he'd left as soon as the two men had come in. Ricky was no longer singing, which was okay since there was no one left who wanted to hear him. Mom wasn't behind the counter anymore. She'd retreated to the kitchen, I suppose. Some moms are like that.

"I'd hate to have to bust you up," the larger man said. He had a thin white scar that ran across his cheek and up to his ear from the corner of his mouth. "I'd do it, though, if you don't come along with us."

I put down the spoon I was using and looked him over. Maybe he could do what he said, maybe not. But he did have a gun. So did Donnie.

"What does he want with me?" I asked, though I had a feeling I knew.

"None of my business," Donnie said. "We just work for him. Get up. Last chance."

"I have to bust you up, it'll make a real mess in here," the larger man said, indicating the interior of Mom's with a wave of his hand. "Mom won't like it. Be hard for you to get a bowl of chili in here again."

I thought about telling him I wouldn't miss the chili, but he wouldn't care, so I didn't mention it. I pushed myself away from the table and stood up.

"Let's go," I said. What difference did it make, anyway?

The big guy looked relieved. The One-Eyed Man wouldn't have liked it if there'd been a disturbance in a public place.

"I knew you'd see the light," the big guy said. He came around the table and touched my elbow. "C'mon. The car's outside."

I shook off his hand. "What, you couldn't bring it in?"

"Always the smart-ass," Donnie said at my back. "You never learn."

He was right about that, I guess. I went outside with them. A long black Lincoln was parked about halfway down the block. Nobody had to tell me that was their car. The One-Eyed Man had a fleet of them. My cab was parked not far away. It was a nice day in late spring, not yet too hot, and somewhere birds were probably singing. Not around Mom's, however.

They walked me to the car, where we stopped while they patted me down. They didn't find anything. Donnie got behind the wheel, and the big guy and I got in the back.

"Just to keep you company," he said as Donnie started the car and pulled away from the curb.

We hadn't gone but a couple of blocks before I realized we weren't headed in the right direction. Donnie knew where he was going. He didn't make mistakes.

"You're headed the wrong way," I said.

"Nah," the big guy said. "We got our orders. The One-Eyed Man's having a picnic in the country."

I was starting to sweat. "That doesn't sound like him."

"What can I tell you? He said he needed some fresh air."

He didn't even try to be convincing. I edged toward the door on my side. That's when I noticed that the handle had been removed. The big guy pulled out his pistol and pointed it at me.

"Just sit still. We'll be there in a little while."

That's what I was afraid of, but I didn't see much that I could to about it other than letting him shoot me while we were in the car. At least that way, they'd have a big cleanup job on their hands.

It didn't take us long to get out of town. We drove for a little way on the blacktop, nobody saying anything, and then Donnie pulled off onto a little dirt road.

"See?" the big guy said. "A picnic."

"Sure," I said. "I'll bet there's a good spot not far down the road. Birds singing, no ants."

"You got it," the big guy said.

Donnie started to whistle between his teeth. I tried to identify the song. Maybe it was supposed to be "Hello, Mary Lou," but Donnie had never been a Ricky Nelson fan as far as I knew. While I was puzzling it out, Donnie turned onto another road, this one not much more than a lane, two dusty ruts that came to a dead end in a little grove.

"Where's the picnic?" I said.

"They must not be here yet," the big guy said.

He opened his door and got out, keeping his gun pointed at me. Donnie got out, too. He came around the front of the car and joined his pal.

"You can get out now," Donnie said.

I was sweating a lot now, but I tried not to let them see how nervous I was. And scared. I was scared, too, plenty scared. I got out of the car, and for a second I thought my knees wouldn't hold me up. They did, though, and I stood there looking around. A little breeze rattled the leaves in the trees, and I heard some kind of bird calling. I didn't know what kind it was, not that it mattered.

The big guy gestured with his pistol. "Walk over that way," he said. "To the trees."

"I don't think so."

"Go ahead," Donnie said. "It's not like you have a choice."

"Donnie," I said. "You're my brother."

"Better you than me," he said. He'd always been like that. "Walk."

It was a nice day. Did I mention that? Clear blue sky, a few little clouds. A really nice day. I turned about and walked toward the trees.

"Why?" I said.

"You know why."

I stopped walking, but I didn't turn around. "Tell me anyway."

"The One-Eyed Man doesn't like it when somebody plays hanky-panky with Peg."

Peg was the One-Eyed Man's wife. She was a black-haired beauty with a roving eye. The One-Eyed Man had trouble keeping her at home.

"He should've sent Peg on this picnic," I said.

"Not a chance," Donnie said.

"Would it do any good if I said I never even met her?"

"No," Donnie said. "It wouldn't. Now walk."

I walked. I didn't know what else to do.

I hadn't gone far when the bullet hit me in the back of my head and slammed me into darkness.

\*\*\*

Donnie was always the strange one. When I'd been a kid, I'd read stories about fairies stealing babies and replacing them with changelings. I thought for a while that's what had happened with Donnie. He was a bully with the smaller kids in school, and he kicked the cat when he thought nobody was looking. How could he be my brother? But we looked so much alike that I finally discarded the changeling idea.

Later on he got into all kinds of trouble. He stole from the lockers at school. He lied to our parents, and he lied to his teachers. Little lies, big lies, it didn't matter to Donnie. He just lied. He robbed a liquor store. He didn't get caught, but I knew. His friends talked to me. I didn't turn him in. He was my brother, even if I still couldn't figure out what was wrong with him.

He was hell with the women. He treated them like dirt or worse, but they flocked to him, anyway. I did okay, but nothing like Donnie. He knocked up a couple of girls in high school, so the stories went. He never told me. We hardly talked after we were ten. He hated me. I never knew why.

Then a few years ago I saw a movie called *The Bad Seed*. Maybe that was Donnie's story. He just happened to be conscience-less, not that he'd ever killed anybody like the girl in the movie did. Not that I knew of at the time.

Not long after that, he tried to kill me.

It was late one night, just about time for me to call it a day, when I got a call that somebody needed a cab on Biloxi Street. It wasn't a bad part of town, but there was some construction going on and the area was pretty deserted. I thought at first I'd just ignore the call. It hadn't been a great day, though, and I figured I might as well pick up a few bucks, so I drove on over.

The street where I was supposed to make the pick-up was dark. I didn't think much of it at the time, but now I'm sure someone, most likely Donnie, had shot out the streetlight. I was about in the middle of the block when a black car roared out of a garage in the building opposite me. On the other side of me was a condemned building that was scheduled to be demolished.

The black car t-boned my cab and shoved it into the wall of the building, which collapsed on me, not that I knew it. I was already unconscious, with broken bones and a serious open head wound. I didn't wake up for a week.

The cops said the car that hit me had been stolen an hour or so before the accident, and there was no way they'd ever find out who'd been driving it.

"Your parents died in a car wreck, didn't they?" one of the cops said. He looked bored by the whole thing.

"Yeah," I told him. "They did."

"A hell of a thing, you almost getting killed the same way."

"It wasn't the same," I said, and it wasn't. My parents had died because the old hoopie my dad had been driving got out of control and went into the wrong lane and hit an eighteen-wheeler. It had never been considered anything but an unfortunate accident, but now I wondered. Cut brake lines? Fiddling with the steering linkage? I wouldn't have put it past Donnie. He hated our parents even more than he hated me.

The cops asked me if I had any idea who'd try to kill me, but I told them I didn't know. That I didn't have an enemy in the world. They could ask anybody. I don't know if they even bothered.

What I said was the truth. I didn't have any enemies. Just a brother. In the second before the car hit me, I'd turned and seen Donnie's face through the windshield. Yes, it was dark, and the car didn't have its lights on, but it was Donnie behind the wheel. I knew it in my broken bones.

The doctors kept me around for a while and had a psychologist talk to me a few times. He said something about brain damage, but I felt okay. There was nothing wrong with my head. Donnie was the crazy one.

Donnie never came to see me in the hospital, not that I'd expected him to, and not long after that he got a job with the One-Eyed Man. I'd seen him only a couple of times since then, but only from a distance. He didn't try to kill me again. He was biding his time, I suppose, until he could shoot me in the back of the head. Maybe that was more satisfying to him. More personal.

***

It was a long time before I opened my eyes again. I wasn't sure where I was or what had happened at first. When I tried to sit up, my head felt as if somebody was inside of it trying to get out. That brought things back to me.

I spit dirt and grit out of my mouth and turned over on my back, but that was as far as I got. I lay there for awhile, looking at the sky through slitted eyes. It was getting on toward late afternoon, I thought. After a while I put a hand to my head. There was a good bit of blood—scalp wounds are like that—but I wasn't dead. Not yet, anyway.

Donnie didn't know it, but while I was in the hospital after he'd tried to kill me the first time, they'd had to put a metal plate in my head to replace the part of my skull I'd lost. Donnie's bullet had hit the metal plate and skidded across my head. I might be a mess, but I'd live.

Too bad for Donnie that he hadn't checked me out and put a bullet in me just to make sure I was dead. Overconfidence. Just one of his many faults.

I held my hand in front of my face and folded two fingers under my thumb. I could see that only two fingers were sticking up. Two times two was four. I could remember that, too. That meant I was okay, didn't it?

I tried to stand. It took me a while, but I made it to my feet. Walking was a little harder, but I managed to shuffle along. When I got to the rutted road, I got into one of the ruts and headed back to the blacktop. It was slow going.

At the blacktop I had to stop. I couldn't go any farther. No use even to try. So I stood at the side of the road and stuck up a thumb. It wasn't a busy road. A few cars passed me by, but finally an old pickup stopped.

The driver took a look at me and said, "You look bad, son."

"Wrecked my car in a field over there," I said, making a vague gesture. "Need to get back town."

He thought it over. "You can ride in the bed. Don't want no blood on my seats."

"That's fine. I need another favor."

"What's that?"

I gave him my address and asked if he could take me there.

"Hospital do you more good."

"I'm okay. How about it?"

He said it wasn't too much out of his way, so I thanked him and went around to the back of his truck. I let the tailgate down and got in. It wasn't hard. I just lay down and slid.

I felt every bump and rattle of the road as we headed back to town, and every one of them made me think of Donnie. He could always say he was doing what his boss told him to do, nothing personal. It might even have been true. That didn't mean he wouldn't try again.

When we got to my house, the pickup stopped. I slid out and shuffled to the door and went inside. It was getting dark by then, but I didn't turn on the lights. I went into the bedroom, lay down on the bed, and went to sleep. I didn't dream.

***

I spent a couple of days sleeping. I got up to drink some water now and then and to use the bathroom. Didn't do much else. Nobody would say anything about me being missing. The cab was mine, and it'd be a while before it was towed. The One-Eyed Man probably had that covered, anyway.

After another day or two my head finally cleared up as much as it ever did, and I thought some more about Donnie. And about me. Donnie had tried to kill me twice and failed. The next time I might not be so lucky. Something had to be done about him, and about the One-Eyed Man, as well.

I figured it was time to go see the One-Eyed Man. Seeing me would be a surprise for him, and not the good kind. Maybe I'd give him a heart attack. That should solve the problem.

I knew a little about him. I knew where he went during the day, for one thing. He kept guys like Donnie and his big friend close by, so I'd have to be careful, but I could get to him. I hoped.

I had a couple of spare wigs, so I got one out and put it on. A glance in the mirror told me that it looked okay. Good enough for a visit to the One-Eyed Man, anyway.

***

I've always liked lumberyards. I like the smell of the pine boards and the shavings. I like the way the lumber's laid out in the racks, everything in its place. Nice and orderly. The One-Eyed Man must've liked lumberyards, too, since that's where he holed up.

The place was called Lumber City, and it wasn't one of those big national chains. It was an old-fashioned kind of place, locally owned and operated. That's because nobody messed with the One-Eyed Man. Anybody who did got taken out in the country and shot. Well, maybe not that, exactly, but something equally bad. It didn't matter if you drove a cab or represented a business with profits more than the gross national product of a small country.

I was going to mess with him, however, because he'd already messed with me. I was supposed to be dead, anyway, so why not?

Lumber City took up about a quarter of a block, and it backed up to an open graveled space of about fifty yards that separated it from railroad tracks. Down by the tracks were some old wooden warehouses that had been abandoned twenty or more years ago.

I walked to the area from my house. It took me a while, but I didn't see anybody I knew or anybody that even had an interest in me. I went into in one of the warehouses through a doorway that hadn't held a door for a long time. The place had been used by squatters for a while, and paper and trash were scattered all around. The squatters were gone. A musty smell hung in the air, the rats and feral cats and scavenged everything perishable, so the odor wasn't rank. I didn't see any cats, but I scared off a few rats when I entered.

For about fifteen minutes I watched Lumber City. There wasn't a lot of activity. A couple of men loaded lumber onto a flatbed truck and drove off, but that was all. I went back outside and walked across the gravel to the chain-link fence that blocked the way. The fence ran along three sides of the lumberyard, so I had to get over it or go through the front. Going through the front wasn't an option. At least there was no razor wire on top of the fence.

Climbing the fence wasn't easy, but I got over. I dropped a couple of feet to the ground and jarred my head a little more than I liked, but that was okay. The bad feeling passed quickly. Nobody saw me, or if anybody did, nobody cared. The One-Eyed man didn't worry a lot about people sneaking up on him.

I walked along one of the aisles of lumber until I came to the building. There was a stairway on the side leading to a door. I walked up the steps to the little wooden landing, opened the door, and walked in.

I'd hoped the room behind the door would be empty, but it wasn't. Two men sat in straight-backed chairs. One of the men faced me. The other faced the broad open stairway that came up from the first floor where the customers were. Or would've been if there'd been any customers.

"Don?" the man facing me said. He wore a white shirt with "Bob" stitched over the pocket. He also wore a shoulder holster with a .45 automatic in it.

"I'm here to see the One-Eyed Man."

The other man turned to look at me. "That's not Don."

His name, according to his shirt, was Cole, and he also had a .45 in a shoulder rig.

"Who is he, if he's not Don?" Bob asked.

Cole didn't say anything. I didn't say anything, either. I looked down the stairs at the shelves of nuts and bolts, the racks of window frames, the light fixtures, the ceiling fans. A man stood behind a short counter. He also wore a white shirt but had no gun. The legit customers wouldn't have approved. He looked up at me without much interest. I couldn't see if his shirt had his name stitched over the pocket.

After about half a minute, Cole said, "You're his brother."

He didn't seem all that surprised to see me alive. The One-Eyed Man wasn't likely to have told anybody he'd had me killed. Or tried to.

"That's right," I said, "and I want to see the One-Eyed Man."

"Mr. Merchant doesn't see people," Bob said.

"Sure he does," I said. I pointed to the door to my left. "He's in that room right now, waiting to see me."

"I don't think so," Cole said.

Both he and Bob were bigger than I am, and when they stood up, they looked even bigger. They started toward me, Bob from the right, Cole from the left. I must have looked pretty harmless, as they didn't bother to pull their pistols.

While I'd hoped the room would be empty, I hadn't counted on it, and I wasn't as harmless as I looked. I reached inside my jacket and drew out a .38 revolver.

"Stop right there," I said.

Cole and Bob stopped. They seemed surprised. The One-Eyed Man must not have many visitors. Especially armed ones.

"I thought you locked that damn door," Cole said.

"I thought you did," Bob said.

"Never mind that," I said. "It wasn't locked, and that's that. Let's go see the One-Eyed Man."

"He's not gonna like it."

"You never can tell. Let's go."

We went, Bob in the lead, followed by Cole and me. When Bob opened the door, I saw a room that didn't look like part of the lumberyard, though I suppose some of it might have come from there. The walls were knotty pine, and the floors were polished hardwood. The big desk was cherry wood, and the overstuffed chairs were upholstered in leather dyed almost the same color as the desk.

We entered the room, and I kicked the door closed behind me. The One-Eyed Man sat behind the desk. He looked like the guy in the shirt ads, hair graying at the temples, a big black patch over his right eye. He wore a blue short-sleeved shirt with a maroon time. No jacket.

"Don?" he said.

"I'm not Don," I said. "Put your hands on top of the desk. Bob and Cole, you two have a seat."

They didn't argue, and neither did the One-Eyed Man. They sat in the chairs while the One-Eyed Man put his hands on the desk and looked me over.

"You're the crazy brother."

"Crazy?" I said. What was he talking about? "If I was crazy, I'd just shoot you. I might, anyway. After all, that's what you did to me, or what you had done. You didn't even give me a chance to explain."

He didn't look scared. "Explain? What's there to explain? You were boinking my wife. I don't stand for that." He paused. "Why aren't you dead?"

"I'm hard to kill. Donnie should've told you that."

"He didn't have the heart to go through with it."

"Oh, he did it, all right. It just didn't work out."

"Maybe he'll get another chance."

"I hope so, because this time I have a gun, too. I'd like to ask you something first, though."

The One-Eyed Man shrugged. "Tell me, then."

"Who told you I was boinking your wife?"

"It wasn't Don, if that's what you're thinking?"

"I didn't think Donnie told you. He's too smart for that. Was it Cole, here, or Bob?"

The two men in the chairs glared at me. I didn't mind.

"It wasn't them. A couple of people saw you out with her."

"Yeah. I'm sure they did. In public places, too, I'll bet. You really think I'm that stupid?"

He must have, but he didn't say so. He just sat there.

"It was Donnie," I said. "How would I meet your wife? He's the one who was close to you. He's the one who could get to know her."

The One-Eyed Man thought about that for a second. Then he said, "Go on."

"He tried to kill me in a car accident," I said, "but that didn't work. So he figured he'd get you to kill me for him. Everybody knows how you feel about your wife. Donnie's smooth, and he could fool her. Others, too. People might think it was me she was with, especially if he wanted them to."

"The nose," the One-Eyed Man said. "Yours is broken."

"Who notices a nose?" I said. "Donnie probably got your wife to use my name when they were out. He could do that. And before long I'm a dead man. Problem solved for both of you. Or that's what you'd think."

"He told me you were dead."

"Donnie's always been a liar, but this time he was just mistaken."

"About what?" Donnie said, coming into the room behind me.

I'd been expecting him or someone like him. I knew the One-Eyed Man would have a button under the desk that he pushed if he needed help. He'd done that before he put his hands on the desk, or maybe it worked when he stepped on it. Didn't matter.

"Hello, Donnie," I said, turning to face him.

"Son of a bitch," he said.

He had a pistol ready, but he was too surprised to fire it. Even at that his finger was tightening on the trigger when I shot him. The bullet hit him about in the middle of his face on that unbroken nose of his. I was pretty sure he didn't have a metal plate there. Some of the back of his head came off. I was glad I wouldn't have to clean up the place.

I turned back around before he fell and made sure that Cole and Bob and the One-Eyed Man didn't jump me.

"You don't have to worry about Donnie and your wife anymore," I told the One-Eyed Man. "Are we square or do I have to pull the trigger again?"

"You're sure it was Donnie with Peg?"

What did he think I'd say? "I'm sure."

"We're square, then."

"Fine. I'll be going."

The room smelled of gun smoke and blood. I didn't look down at Donnie as I left. I went down the stairs and out the front door. The clerk didn't seem to notice that I was even there. He must have been used to a little gunfire now and then.

***

I never saw anything in the papers about Donnie's body being discovered. I didn't expect to. I figured it was in some river or lake somewhere, weighed down by some concrete blocks from the lumberyard. The thought of the fish nibbling on Donnie's toes didn't bother me a bit.

My cab had been towed and impounded, but I bailed it out and went back to driving. I got some good fares and some not so good. Like my days. I'd have headaches now and then, bad ones. I blamed Donnie for that, but I got over them. Donnie wouldn't get over what had happened to him. His own fault, though.

It was a little over a month before Peg called me. Her voice was husky. She said she was sorry about my brother.

"Don't worry about it," I told her. "He tried to kill me twice. I had to do something."

She sighed. "I suppose so."

Peg and I had met when I'd picked her up one night, just another fare. She'd been out with friends the One-Eyed Man approved of, but they'd gotten sloppy drunk, and she'd walked out on them. We talked a little as I drove her, and we'd hit it off. We'd managed to meet a few times after that, and we'd been careful not to be seen. Or so we thought. Someone had seen us though, and had reported to the One-Eyed Man.

"When am I going to see you again?" she asked.

I thought about the bullet hitting the back of my head. I thought about Donnie, under water and cold as stone.

"Soon," I said, and hung up the phone.

# Dark Harvest
## by Thomas A. Crowell, Esq.

The sound of gunfire woke me up.
I drank my breakfast neat:
Old bourbon in my coffee cup.
Sirens wailed on down the street.

I parted the Venetian blinds
And let the headlights in.
This city's full of one-track minds,
With all tracts growing sin.

Feel like a farmer, not a cop—
The streetlight is my sun.
Night crimes: they are my bumper crop.
Death sprouts from each drawn gun.

Cool greenbacks of a gambler's swag,
I pluck like tender shoots.
Red blossoms from each body bag,
All bloom from ill-reputes.
I pack my loaded gun and shield;
My veins are full of ice.
I prowl along my pavement-field:
It's time to harvest vice.

# Homicide Duty Ain't for the Lonely
## by Thomas A. Crowell, Esq.

I flashed my badge.
She flashed her smile.
A bold black widow, she had style.

She dropped her gun.
I dropped my pants.
We lost ourselves in Satan's dance.

She changed her dress.
I changed my mind.
I guess it's still an unsolved crime …

# Frankford Avenue
## by Melanie Dante

Sweet nothings
Dirty tidings
In motion
Dualities dance
Midnight moments
Make the jaded heart grow fonder
If only a bit of trust can fill that
Desolate lonely place
So demure so impenetrable
A detour into a maze
Mutually conflicted intentions
Momentarily mended
In a near insatiable set of needs
Too vulgar to discuss in public
Dissolved down through a filter of wonder lust
As love lasts long
Into the dark passage of the night
Then—Dawn
Lying naked
By the open window
Looking out amidst a slight breeze
Infinite concrete and metal
Soft sounds of sleep
Soothingly defined rhythmic breath
Combined heartbeat
Comfort found inside
Confines of control

All dissipates into haze
Clouded sunlight and traffic
At the break of day
Little is left to know

Ashes line fluid stains on sheets
The smell of fresh sweat turning stale
A contradiction to the senses
Sweet nothings dissolved away
Watered down drinks
Fresh rain hitting the filth of the city streets …

# Rothko's Daughter
## by Richard Godwin

I FOLLOWED HER, HAVING nowhere else to go. She was shining like a wax doll under the bus shelter lights, looking like she'd melt. I sat down next to her and lit a Marlboro, feeling the drops of rain crawl down my face like insects.

"Has the last one been?" I said.

"The last bus left a long time ago," she whispered.

A woman like her exists only in metaphor. She converted reality as easily as I picked pockets.

I looked at the money I'd stolen from Hank. I didn't want to go back to the flat. I was running out of time that night, tired of seeing the same faces. The crowd I knew conformed to the idea of a rebellious life. We all propped up each others' lies. And I felt exposed. Even my walk had the soiled predictability of a thief.

My reflection in the shelter sickened me. I stole a glance at her, wondering what her name was. She had a defiled mystery about her. Even now, I consider her iconic.

"Didn't I see you the other night in the club?" I said.

"You mean Mirage?"

"Yeah, that's right."

"I remember kissing you."

"You do?"

She leaned towards me.

"I could use some downers."

We listened to the rain washing the pavements, just two users with mutual recognition between us as midnight fell beyond the hollow rooftops. Nothing seemed real in those days, the small corner of London I inhabited looked like a stage set. Everyone I knew was a facade, an empty mouth muttering words that made no sense anymore. It was all about to change.

"I know where I could score some," she said. "Don always has good gear."

She put her faded denim jacket over her head and we ran through the sodden streets, stopping outside an electrical shop. She pressed the intercom and we were buzzed in.

I followed her up some stairs to a studio. Don was standing in the middle of the room surrounded by clear plastic bags with pills in them. Clothes were strewn everywhere. There were two large frames on the wall which were turned round so their backs were facing forward. Someone had written, "Do not reflect me," on the back of one in bright pink ink. Don was wearing only a pair of silver trousers. There were two long gashes on his chest. He'd been crying and his mascara had run.

"That bastard did this to me, Sam's been screwing around again."

"You need to get that looked at," she said.

"By who? My injuries can't be assessed by a doctor. I'm losing my definition by the day. What do you see when you look at me?"

She laid her hand on his shoulder.

"I see my friend, Don."

"We trade. That's all we do. I know about being used, I know what it feels like to be a hole." He started removing his lipstick with a dirty rag. "We're all strangers, peer behind the veneer. We make ourselves up until we can't anymore."

She walked over to one of the frames and turned it round.

"Look at yourself in the mirror," she said.

Don raised a hand.

"I don't want to see him."

"Who?"

"That person claiming to be me."

"Look at your chest."

"No."

"You don't want to get an infection."

"We're all infected. Take me naked as I am."

"You'll get scars."

"Then I'll make sure everyone sees them, what he did to me."

His gut wobbled as he wandered across the room and struggled into a Miami shirt.

She cupped her hand over my ear.

"He self-harms, Sam ran away years ago."

I watched as Don rummaged through a drawer, lifting out forks and holding them up to the light. He laid them down on a small table, then picked a bag up from the floor. I handed him the cash and he passed me the downers.

"What's with the forks?" I said.

Don tossed his hair back.

"Who is this guy?"

She pecked him on the cheek, and I followed her outside.

"We could go to my place and sleep, I found some tins of soup," she said.

"Found?"

"In an open van."

"I don't even know your name."

"Florence. You?"

"Jack."

On the way there I kept thinking she didn't look like Florence. I knew all about the city of art, and I thought she was trying to dignify herself in some way. I'd never kissed her until that night. She made it up, the scene at the club. I liked that sense of corruption about her. She was well within my grasp.

Her one room flat stood over a hardware store and smelt of stale air and cheap perfume. The walls were lined with pictures. I looked at one in which she was tattooing an enormous man.

"That was a big piece," she said.

"You're a tattoo artist?"

"I own my own parlour."

"You're good."

She slapped me on the chest.

"Hey, that's how I can pay you back, Jack. I can give you a tattoo."

We took the downers and smoked dope.

She waved her arm in the direction of the tiny kitchen area.

"Help yourself to some food."

Her fridge contained a bottle of Smirnoff and a slice of rotting cheddar. I found two buckled tins of tomato soup in a cupboard full of light bulbs.

"I know where I can get you some crack," I said.

She was lying on the floor, and she looked at me with the momentary hope of the damned. I knew the look. It existed in the faces of all the sad women I'd exchanged for one another.

I studied the pictures as the downers kicked in.

"I've been doing it for years," she said. "I'm good with needles."

"You really are, these are some of the best tattoos I've seen. You should be famous."

There were tears in her eyes as she stood up.

"Do you want to know a secret?"

"Sure."

"I'm Rothko's daughter."

"You mean the artist?"

"Yeah, him."

She shoved a heavy book across the floor. I opened it and stared at the images. They just looked like lines of paint on squares. I'd always thought that kind of art was a con, aimed at all the pretentious people who have soirees, fuck each other's wives, and talk about which plays they go to.

"I'm part Russian," Florence said.

"Florence Rothko. It has a ring to it."

She shook her head.

"Florence Dimes. My mother was a nightclub entertainer, she was so beautiful he couldn't resist her."

"You mean a stripper?"

"No, a cabaret artist, she was sophisticated, Jack."

"Have you ever been to a soiree?"

"I did once, I had this dress."

She made a gesture with her hands. Her eyes were heavy, and she stumbled to the floor. I looked at her lying against the sofa, her face broken and lost.

"Did I tell you about the time he took me to New York?"

"No."

"I'll show you the pictures. That's where I get it from, my ability with needles."

"You must have it in your veins."

"What?"

"His artistic temperament."

"That's it, Jack, you understand me. My skin's a canvas. The first time I got a tattoo, I thought, this is the real meaning of penetration.

The needle's entering my body, but it's leaving something beautiful behind."

She shut her eyes. I could see them dart around beneath her eyelids as she slept. I'd watched her sleep before on the night bus, dozing against the window. I followed her on. Her bag lay open beside her on the broken seat. I stole her phone to ring my dealer and listened to her messages. There was a long one from a guy called Mick.

"You're a hideous fraud," he said.

Then he yelled so much he made my ear ache and I threw her phone across the street, where it smashed against a lamp post. I was out of pills that night. I remember falling asleep at the back of a shop selling futons, seeing her face, wanting more from her. I lied about seeing her in the club; I'd never even been to Mirage. I lied to her about most things. That was what I liked about her the most; she was such a willing accomplice.

I studied her on the floor of her littered flat. I didn't understand her, I didn't care. I just wanted to watch my wax doll melt. Her skin had the pallor of an icon. She didn't deserve to have that. She was no better than me. I wanted to show her who she was.

I read the book about her famous father. It talked about his theories and how he was influenced by Nietzsche. It said Rothko died in 1970, which would have made him in his late sixties when he impregnated her mother. I slammed the book shut and woke her. She took a pair of retro glasses out of her bag and put them on. They made her look middle aged. She began looking for something in a drawer as I took my shoes off and went over to the bed. A picture of a man with slicked back hair stared at me out of a corroded silver frame.

"That's my ex," she said. "The asshole, he never gave me any money when he left and now he's shacked up with some bird."

"A man like that can't appreciate an artist like you."

"Jack, that's exactly right."

She fished a CD out of the drawer and put it on.

"Do you like Edith Piaf?"

"I was reading about your father."

"You know he struggled with the label of abstract painter? He said it was like arguing with your parents, that in the end you have to recognise your roots."

"People in that world talk bullshit. I know, my old man's an art critic."

"That's not the same, critics prey on artists. Rothko hated and distrusted them. They think they can define people, and tell us what makes great art, but they don't understand it."

"Rothko might have thought we're connected to our roots, but I'm nothing like my father."

"Maybe not in the way you think you are, but it will come out in some other way. Look at me and the needles I paint with. Rothko's alive in my tattoos. It's all about perception, Jack. Painters show us the way the word really is. You can spend your life not seeing anything, not knowing who anyone really is, because that exists beneath the skin. Did you father really understand art? Could he see someone for what they are, for their unspoken beauty?"

"He belonged to this sick crowd of people who looked down their noses at everyone else. They had their own private little language, just so you knew you were excluded."

"Do you think he loved you?"

I thought about the last time I'd seen him, and the look in his eyes when he found out I'd been stealing.

"There was a lot of fraud surrounding Rothko, that's one of the reasons I don't like the art world."

"That was caused by businessmen ripping him off."

"Why do you think he killed himself?"

"He was misunderstood. He said a painting is permanently impaired by the eyes of the unfeeling."

"A painting doesn't feel anything, it's an object."

"I know what unfeeling eyes can do, Jack."

I looked at her and she was crying, lost in the music, and I held her for a while as she rocked on her little feet. She looked up at me with her mouth half open and I tasted her deceit as she bit my lip and we fell onto the bed. Then I was wiping the tears and the past away as I waited for the dark.

The next morning she said, "Come and get a tattoo, Jack." She handed me her card.

I had no intention of seeing her again. I felt she was tricking me.

I went back to the flat. Hank had gone, taken everything. He'd left me a note.

"Thieves like you belong on the street," it read.

I had a few clothes in a wardrobe. They smelt dank and I stood there trying to remember if Florence had a washing machine. I put them in a black bin liner and looked at the unpaid bills. I couldn't afford the rent. I wanted to move on from the whole stinking place and most of all myself.

I thought I might run into one of the crowd at The Fox and find a place for the night. Instead I saw her ex there. I recognised him from the picture. He was snogging a young blonde guy and I wondered if he'd turned gay after leaving Florence. I began to feel better about myself, having this piece of information. I knew more about her life than she did.

That Saturday afternoon I went to the tattoo parlour, half expecting it not to be there. She was behind the counter reading *Grazia* magazine in the empty shop.

She led me through to the back and I took my shirt off and sat in the chair.

"I figure I'll get my right arm done," I said. "What are you going to do?"

"You'll see."

It hurt, but not as much as losing my self-respect. The pain felt like some physical absolution, and the fact that she was administering it to me filled me with the urge to vandalise her shop. I looked at her face as she stared intently down at her work. The skin was hard beneath her observant eyes. I wanted to ask her about her gay husband. I wanted to find something to hate about her.

I didn't look at it until she finished. She'd drawn a series of lines across a box.

"What is it?"

"It's a Rothko. It's called Magenta, Black."

"I thought you'd do something like a woman or an animal."

"This is better, don't you see, it's worth a lot of money, you've got a replica by Rothko's daughter."

"If I ever need to score I can just hack my arm off and sell it to the nearest art dealer."

She took my head in her hands.

"Don't say that, don't ever say that. I want to be your lover, I need your arms around me, but I've got something missing inside."

She was beautiful and displaced, like a stolen stained glass window, and her body was alive with the kind of sexual disease that turned me on instantly. I held her in my arms as she swayed there in the parlour, the sound of cars hissing on the road outside, and I knew she was an invention. That was what we had in common, our lies. She really was good with needles.

"Do you want to come back with me?" she said. "I'm closing up now."

"I haven't got any pills."

She looked down at the black bin liner. There was a rip in it and a shirt sleeve stuck out.

"You've brought a bag, Jack."

"Just some clothes."

She smiled and I felt like washing. I didn't want to go back with her. I had vertigo in that shop as I glimpsed what I could feel about her if I stayed around. But I needed a place for the night.

She lay down when we got to her flat, and propped her head up on her hand. A lot of her postures looked copied from paintings. I knew all about forgery and theft. That was why I spent those soiled those days with her.

"You can put your things on the sofa," she said.

I felt sad for her then. There can be no permanence for people like us.

"I saw your ex kissing a guy."

She sat up.

"What?"

"He's gay."

"You must be mistaken."

"No, it was him all right."

She started pacing the room.

"Do you know what that bastard said to me? That I knew shit about art. Me!"

"Screw him."

"Let's go there now."

We did. To a derelict basement a few miles away.

He opened the door in a pair of grey Jockeys and said, "I haven't got any."

"I don't want money, Mick."

Florence pushed him aside and marched into the flat. He chased after her and I walked in and watched them fight in the filthy corridor.

"Who you living with?" she said.

"Why do you want to know?"

He had his hands on his hips and she looked over his shoulder into the room behind him.

"Huh," she said, "huh."

There was a young man in the bed; I could see his chest above the sheet. He had this pug face and he kept blinking.

"Too afraid of women now, Mick?" Florence said.

"After you."

She began to march down the corridor towards the front door.

"Come on Jack."

"Even your orgasms are forgeries," Mick shouted after her.

We headed to the nearest bar.

She sat there drinking Martinis, feigning sophistication on stolen money, a tattooed scar on the edge of the broken street.

"Why does it matter?" I said.

"Why does what matter?"

"The fact he's gay, he's not with you anymore."

"But he's not gay, this is all an act put on to make me feel bad, to go back to him."

"Do you think he'd go to those lengths?"

"People do go to lengths Jack, we all want to be seen in a certain way."

"What lengths do you go to, Florence?"

"The lengths I need."

We left the bar and travelled back to her flat.

I felt trapped as she closed the door. She came right up to me so her face was inches from mine. I held her, and she was someone else then in the twilight that fell beyond the window. I searched for her eyes in the room, but she kept them closed, as if the world was too much for her to bear and she wanted to dream. What it was she dreamed I don't know. All I know was that as she touched me and I kissed her face she was shivering. She pushed her hips towards me and gasped.

"I want a baby."

"Do you think your daughter would be like Rothko, too?"

"Come on, I'll show you."

I tried lying, saying all the things she needed me to say. But my face felt like a mask in the dark and I wanted to pull it away and bleed on her, shock her, stop the game that she played better than me. As I tasted the despair in her mouth, I wondered what hatred felt like when it was too old to be born, and lay there inside you holding on like an ancient foetus. I wondered what I'd be like in ten years. And I thought that if she carried my child we'd have to abort it. I'd have to make sure it never saw daylight.

I thought about the time I looked in her handbag while she was sleeping on the bus and that is what it felt like then, inside her as she lay with her eyes shut dreaming of Rothko, conjuring lies. I'd watched her that night at the pale yellow bus shelter. I listened to her talking on her phone. I felt excluded from her conversation. I studied her, so when we spoke it felt natural. That was the advantage I enjoyed. I used to spy on lives and remove things from people I felt they shouldn't own.

I looked at the Rothko she'd inked on my arm as she slept. I was trying to steal money from her purse when she woke.

"Hey, what do you think you're doing?" she said.

"Looking for pills."

"I haven't got any."

She got up and pulled on some clothes.

"You were looking for cash."

"We all steal things, Florence."

"Oh yeah?"

"You've stolen who you are."

She began to punch me with tiny fists and I stood there laughing until she crumpled sobbing to the floor.

"Why don't you put that song on?"

"Do you know why I do tattoos?"

"It's your art."

She stood up and rubbed her eyes.

"That's right."

"What does it feel like being Rothko's daughter?"

"Unwanted and alone."

"But it must be a buzz."

"How can you say that?"

"You're famous."

"I'm not."

"They could write books about you."

"They don't write books about people like me."

"You could be a painter."

"My tattoos hide scars. That's why I got the first one, down here, deep down here, to hide it. Then I got more, because I keep seeing scars everywhere, I want to cover my whole body with tattoos. Don't you think skin's disgusting? I don't want to be a physical object. I want to be one huge Rothko then people can look at me and see."

"See what?"

"What I really am."

"Everyone has skin, Florence."

"Rothko's canvas was his skin."

"What are the scars?"

"Oh, you should know."

"Why?"

"Because you're stained like me."

"Yeah, sure."

She told the truth in a figurative way, the literal was lost on her. The meanings she conveyed felt like tiny fish hooks entering me.

"I'm scarred, I need to be tattooed inside."

"Like you need a baby?"

"I'm told I'll never have one."

I looked at her standing there, and saw how young she was.

"You're not really his daughter are you?"

"How can you say that?"

"You've made yourself look older."

"Are you nuts?"

I picked up her glasses from the night table.

"These have clear lenses in them, you don't need them. You'd have to be ancient to be his, and you're not."

"Get out, get out," she said.

I was going.

Then, as I was by the door she said, "They never wanted me. They never even used to touch me afterwards."

I was holding her for hours before she let me get away. She clutched onto my jacket with mascara-stained fingers and left a print there. It was still there the day I burnt it like a soiled memento.

Florence's real parents had given her away. She told me stuff about her childhood I never want to recall, things that made me hate desire. She asked me for things I would never be able to give and reminded me what I was. She was naked without her lie. I left her at the parlour that night as she began to cover the rest of her body with tattoos.

"Do you understand now?" she said.

"Why Rothko? Why pick him? It could have been any artist."

"Because he's abstract. The truth isn't reality. He colours my stains. He allows me to forget."

"There are other abstract painters. It was a movement."

"Did your father give you that information?"

"Yeah, he did."

"What else did he give you, Jack?"

"Nothing."

"Is that why you have to steal?"

"We're all trying to take a piece of ourselves back."

"You've stripped me to the bone."

"I think he would have liked you."

That was the best I could come up with. As I closed the door she was staring down at her skin with incredulity.

I expected to read about her in the papers, having died from some weird ink poisoning, an indecipherable portrait of suffering by the roadside.

I moved on, but I couldn't erase her memory. I called her at the parlour a few months later, and Florence stayed in touch over the years. She took up painting. She married a guy I used to know. He told her he was an art dealer. I asked him to tell her the truth; I didn't want to know more about her life than she did. She discovered he was dealing drugs when he went to prison. She had several miscarriages and an exhibition called The Meaning of Skin. I got an invitation but I never went. I didn't want to remember who I used to be.

Many years before I met her, I once tried to steal a painting from a gallery. The guard saw me lifting it off the wall, and I ran away. It was by an artist who'd been well reviewed by my father. I thought I could sell it, and get some cash for drugs. I despised the art world. I wanted to gatecrash it and bring it down. Those days I spent with Florence changed that. She removed my desire to trespass in others' lives.

For a while that left me with nothing. I went to visit my father. I hired a suit and listened to him talk about the art world. I'd gone there with a speech prepared about what my life had been. I wanted to make an admission. But all he did was talk, stealing my opportunity. As I was leaving, he asked me what I did. I told him I owned a paint factory and a yacht.

"Are you interested in art?" he said.

"I knew Rothko's daughter."

"Kate?"

"No, Florence."

"I didn't know he had a daughter called Florence."

"You didn't know you had a son called Jack."

He went off to look for an article he'd written which he wanted to show me and I drove away. All the way back to my small flat I tasted the bitter root of hypocrisy. I thought of how I hid from Florence, and exposed her as a forgery. And I realised in doing so I'd robbed myself.

She OD'd soon after her exhibition. She'd lost her home. Some kids found her body in an alley. They were taking pictures of her tattooed legs when the police came.

I still carry the small Rothko she left me with. An art dealer, a real art dealer I sold some coke to years later, said it was a good representation. Florence was a metaphor for too many things. I still remember her for showing me the complex beauty of deceit.

# The Other Man's Wife
## by Richard Godwin

Sulphurous streetlights flickered in the broken wind
That drove Rex Carver down Crescent Boulevard
As he wrapped his trench coat around his ravenous bones.
Dead leaves slapped the darkened windowpanes of peeling houses,
While the gale's rage was ruptured by the looming gasworks
That stared blackly down at the town called Desecration.
The factory held a crane shot into hell, as the wild air broke around
    the derelict edifice,
Snatching debris from the littered pavement and blasting it into Rex's
    stinging eyes.

A rusted gutter burst in the curtain of rain, and the dripping cell
That had been his home flashed back into Rex's mind.
He clutched her memory in his sweating palm
Like a sepia snapshot that was a key to the past,
Like a scarcely shackled chain or a broken hinge
That barely kept the door shut to the room he dreaded entering.
There was no moon overhead, for he'd lost it
When the doors slammed shut and he tried to forget the bitter taste of
    betrayal.

Beyond the creeping street shadows her face polluted the black sky.
In his room at the cheap hotel Rex knelt by the stained bed
And held his hands in supplication.
But instead of prayer the word revenge broke like a blister from his
    parched lips.
"Her name is treachery and I am in Desecration again," he screamed.

The city took its name from events a century before
When looters violated every wife who lived there,
Engendering the legend no woman in Desecration would ever have
    a heart.

That night Rex left his room in search of whisky and travelled
    there,
To the unlit house in Temptation Street at the edge of town. He
    pressed his finger to the bell,
Knowing that a hundred years of violation wouldn't wash away the
    pain.
His vows to walk a law-abiding path crumbled at the distant chime
That echoed within the house like someone singing in a storm.
He left and walked the wasteland of factories and empty tenements,
Passing stricken forms crying out for mercy.
"There is none," Rex said, "the forlorn have only loss."

A blind woman clutched at his tattered sleeve on Crescent
    Boulevard.
"Help me," she said, the words foaming on her crusted lips.
"Did she put you in the frame too?" Rex said.
The woman turned her opaque eyes to him. "Who do you mean?"
"Evangeline, melody of hate, valley of forbidden knowledge, the
    poisoned apple."
"Did you say her name is vengeance?" she said. "Yes," Rex said, "yes."
He returned there the second night,
To the house plush with the trappings of crime.

He walked into the grey hallway and she stood there
In her skin of a black satin dress,
Her fingers delicately wrapped around the slender cigarette holder
Like the poisoned tendrils of some exotic vine.
"Rex, so you're out," she said, her words full of smoke.
"I thought I'd pay you a visit."
"Whisky right?" she said in the old way, as if barely a day had
    passed.
"Double on the rocks."

She sat watching him and he told her of his hopes.
"I can get you work," she said.
"I make my own money."
He heard the sound of a trap bending against its spring
As she rose and walked over to him,
Laid a cold hand on his shoulder,
And pierced his skin with the slender hook of arousal.
"Let me help you Rex, after all," a mocking smile wavered on her
burgundy lips.

She left him there and went upstairs.
Rex stayed close to the ticking clock,
Its wooden case like a coffin which housed a metronome but no melody.
Its rhythm said, 'Desire is stronger than revenge.'
He knew she was alone, for there was no car on the drive.
The gunshot drove him up the stairs, back to when it happened.
He smelt the smoke before he saw her on the bed in the same position
She'd used to lure him to her before. This time there was no body on
the floor.

As she laid the silver Derringer down Rex thought her hands were
dealing a deck
And each card bore his name on it. 'I'll take the piece,' he said,
lifting it from the bed.
He touched her and stepped into the portrait she'd etched of the
original scene
When the shot blasted the night. He'd thought she was dead,
Finding her alive, he made her guilt his own.
"Come to me Rex," she said, drawing back the sheets.
They lay in the post-coital night discussing ways
Of making money now that he was on the straight and narrow.

"You said you'd wait for me Evangeline." "You need a shave," she said,
And fetched her Cut Throat razor, whose blade she sharpened
rhythmically on the strop,
Which made a noise like the skinning of an animal.
She shaved Rex as close to the bone as cutting without killing would
allow.

"He'll employ you," she said, "he doesn't know my past."
And so he got to work for Eddy,
Her small mean husband with no sparkle in his eyes, who spoke in
    clipped orders.
Rex saw she hated him and knew what dark task he was being
    commissioned with.

"You killed your first husband," he said.
"I marry ugly propositions."
"And I took the rap. What will you trade with when your beauty
    fades?"
"Do I look older Rex?"
"Not by a single day."
Rex ignored her homicidal heart,
Enjoying long silken afternoons in her bed,
Where he searched her skin in vain for scars.

He didn't think too much about
The cruel lines around her eyes,
Nor her habit of sitting in the shadows.
Her hair felt like gossamer, her flesh was flawless.
And Eddy lorded it over his staff
With the nonchalance of a man who did away
With those who displeased him. Rex wondered why he wasn't
    chagrined
By a wife who showed him no warmth.

It was less her feral smell than the manner in which her eyes
    avoided his
That handed Rex the piece of knowledge
Which traded Evangeline for vengeance
And all its dark strictures.
In her bedroom he tasted the bitter root of desire and knew she had
    none.
He steadied himself on the cracked washbasin in the bathroom,
And his face in the tarnished mirror said, "You would have your
    pleasure with her.
Well she will eat you this time, and leave only feathers and bones."

Alone one morning drinking coffee in her darkened room,
As Eddy travelled on business
With his guns and hired men
Bearing suitcases full of stained cash,
He asked her if she wanted a future with him
And she looked away, towards the azure sky beyond her cold window.
"I don't believe in it Rex, do you?"
"Yes I do, I do," he said, his fingernails puncturing his palms.

They dined at the Half Moon, the place that blighted lovers frequented
When husbands were away and women wanted to be unseen.
The bistro stood beneath a broken iron bridge
That leaked when it rained and smelt of corrosion.
Next to it was a neon sign that blinked maniacally:
"Life insurance is cheap, death is not."
And Rex noticed she was another woman within the chiaroscuro of
    the neon glow,
A hard and calculated piece of sin bent on gain and torment.

She chose her moment as they ate.
"Rex without him we might have what you want."
"What is it I want if I can't have you Evangeline?"
"You have me in one sense," she said, digging her fork into her
    dripping sirloin.
Her parted lips were moist. "He will find out," he said.
"He won't if you … "
She told him with her eyes the thing she wouldn't say.
Rex dropped his gaze to the blood pooling at the rim of her plate.

He got drunk that night and fumbled with her too roughly in the back
    of the Buick
And she gasped and slapped him with hot animal pleasure.
"I'm not ashamed of desire," he said, mounting her on the worn,
    creaking leather seats,
Unleashing the caged anger of his lust within her flesh.
"I wanted you all the time I was away," he said breathlessly into her ear.
"A little murder will seal the deal."
"I'll do it Evangeline." He raised the hem of her Chianti red dress

And she drew him deep within her beneath the useless iron bridge.

Eddy returned and days passed in which Rex didn't see Evangeline,
Except in the rainwater that collected in the city's gutters.
He satisfied himself elsewhere,
Aware of a distinct lack of jealousy in his soul.
The night he set out from her bedroom with the pistol
Evangeline's eyes looked milky, as if she was full of pleasure
At remembering how she'd used him once
For a crime that was hers alone.

She stroked the loaded chamber of the black Beretta and pulled his
    mouth to hers,
Promising him her body in the stolen hours,
The lost ours where quietness dwells beneath forgotten memory
And blackness hovers at the windowpane.
"I'll give you what you want, Rex."
"You already have, Evengeline."
"I'll give you more."
"What more is there to give?"

Sultry olive skinned Iva Stroud
Saw Rex creep along the garden wall like a shadow.
Eddy's unknown mistress was a lithe and carnal woman
He believed spied his enemies better than his killers did.
And she watched Rex steal into the corridor near the office
Where Eddy was counting cash with wet fingertips.
Outside the office door she held out her hand
And Rex placed the gun in her cool palm and walked away.

He saw Evangeline's face at the window,
A carving in disbelief.
He left the house and gardens in Temptation Street, the scar at the
    edge of Desecration,
And returned to his room where he lay awake
And kissed the neck of a bottle of Chivas Regal,
While Iva scaled the staircase to Evangeline and entering her room
    with the Beretta said,

"He is mine, more mine than he was ever yours,
Did you think to destroy him and what we have?"

Evangeline launched herself at the other woman,
This dark impostor in her plan,
The unknown ingredient in Eddy's machinations,
And a shot rang out so loudly in the still and brooding night
Rex sat bolt upright in bed, spilling the smoky smell of whisky into
  the room,
Knowing she was dead.
And so Eddy married Iva,
The woman who'd ended Evangeline.

He'd kept her well hidden and now displayed her publicly
In low-cut cocktail dresses, his wife,
The woman who'd saved his life.
Eddy boasted about her prowess.
"Iva heard Evangeline talking to some lover on the phone,
Saying she was going to kill me," he said.
"It's her who's dead."
He feasted like a snake on Iva's flesh.

Rex met Iva each afternoon while Eddy ran his crew
And he talked to his lover about their future,
That he'd pulled like a joker from Evangeline's deck.
One evening Eddy ate and collapsed at Iva's feet,
Coughing blood and the dinner she served him onto the floor.
She and Rex left with Eddy's money
And went to live alone, beyond Desecration.
They'd worked it out when Rex was in prison, Iva would be the other
  man's wife.

Rex dwelt on the legend of Desecration
And the lust for the baubles that other men own.
For he found Iva had grown accustomed to betrayal, finding little
  pleasure in fidelity.
She said it was like a hunger for some exotic fruit and the thrill of it
  left her craving more.

"You do understand Rex?" she said.
"I do, I did in prison."
One night as Iva lay sweating with her lover, Rex found a silver
   Derringer in his hand
And he climbed the soiled staircase to their broken bedroom.

# Let's Do Lunch
## by Joseph Goodrich

FOR ALL ITS STATUS as a Hollywood landmark—the place had been around since 1949, eons in California time—Miceli's never seemed to be crowded at lunch.

Larry Wynman liked eating there for that very reason. He could red-pencil a script or work out the details of a budget and rest assured that he wouldn't be bothered over the remains of his chicken Piccanti. Carlo would silently appear every now and again to replenish his wine glass, Loretta might step outside to gaze at the traffic on Las Palmas for the time it took to smoke a cigarette, but there was usually nothing more than that to distract him from the work at hand.

Usually.

*"Lar-r-r-r--y!"*

He glanced up from the script he was reading, and realized immediately that today, Goddamnit, today was going to be different.

A shaggy, overweight figure in dirty jeans and a scuffed leather jacket moved toward him through the red-velvet gloom.

*Rick Turnbull. Goddamnit.*

Larry's father had made a plush living as a grade-Z movie producer, churning out material for the exploitation markets. He'd given a number of writers and directors their first shot at the brass ring—not because he had any special nose for talent, but because hungry, ambitious kids work cheap. Rick Turnbull had been one of those kids. Thirty years ago Sam Wynman, nearing the end of his career (and his life, as it turned out), had bought a script of Rick's. Shot in two weeks, shown at drive-ins across the country, *Trailer Park Tramps* had made a pile of money and been banned in a handful of Bible-Belt states. Sam Wynman couldn't have been more pleased. "Some guys make silk purses out of sow's ears," he'd told *Variety*. "As for me, well, I like sow's ears. And so do a lot of other people. Look at the business *Tramps* is doing, and tell me I'm wrong."

No one told him. Or if they did, he didn't give a damn. The three B's (breasts, bikes, and blood) had served Sam well and he wasn't about to abandon them. Films like *House of Harlots*, *Cat Fight* and *Blood Beast* had bought the house in Beverly Hills and the wives to go along with the house; *Screw-Ball* had paid for Larry's Ivy-League education. Everyone liked Sam but no one respected him. It should come as no surprise, perhaps, that when Larry moved into the industry himself, he thirsted after prestige, acclaim, "quality" … In short, silk purses.

Rick Turnbull was definitely not silk-purse material. He hadn't had a script optioned, much less produced, in years. How he made a living was anyone's guess; he worked in a bookstore, maybe, or drove a cab, or cleaned swimming pools—one scenario was as plausible as another. He'd done a stint in Camarillo State Hospital, driven into psychosis by liquor and pills. The days of coking and toking were supposedly long past, but so was any vestige of a career. Larry viewed him with all of the disdain the winners in LA feel for the losers. And with all of the unspoken, unacknowledged fear, as well: *Please, God, don't let this happen to me.*

*Rick Turnbull. Goddamnit.*

Rick huffed up to the table and stuck out a moist hand. "*Larry.* Good to *see* you."

Larry gave the proffered paw an unwilling shake. "Rick. Hello."

"Mind if I join you?"

"Well, I'm expecting a friend in—" Larry glanced at his Rolex, "—in a couple of minutes, so—"

"A couple of minutes is all I need, Larry." Rick eased his bulk into the other chair, then tapped the script Larry had set down. "What's this?"

"Oh … Just something I'm looking at."

"What is it? What's it about?—Wait, let me guess. I look into my crystal ball, and I see … I see … A thriller."

"How the hell did you know that?" Larry said, startled.

"So I'm right? It's a thriller?"

"Yeah. It is."

"Psychological? Sexy? Literate?"

"Well—*yeah*."

"I hate to tell you, Larry, but sexy, literate, psychological thrillers are out. No one gives a rat's ass for sexy, literate, psychological thrillers these days. That's not what the people want. I'll tell ya what they want. What they *want* … " Rick put his elbows on the table and leaned forward. " … Is horror," he whispered.

"Horror," Larry echoed.

"Look at the box office, man. Horror's big."

"You're not telling me anything I don't know."

"Then why are you wasting your time on sexy, literate, psychological *crap* like this?"

"How do you know it's crap? You haven't read it."

"I don't need to. I'll tell ya right now it won't make a cent. You need a horror movie. A horror movie, Larry."

"I *hate* horror movies."

"You hate money, too? You're so rich now you don't want to make a little more?"

"That's not the point."

"Sam wouldn't have said that."

"Leave my father out of this, Rick."

"All I'm trying to do is tell ya where the action is."

"I don't need *you* to tell me *anything*," Larry bristled. "I happen to have some idea of what sells. I *work* in this town, Rick—which is more than I can say for you. All right?"

Rick's eyes clouded with hurt, and Larry realized that he'd gone too far.

"Look," Larry said, hating himself for trying to make nice, "maybe you're right. Maybe I should I make a horror movie. I don't know. What I do know is that *this*," he gestured at the script, "is what I've got. I've put a lot of time and money into this project. And you want me to just drop it?"

"Yeah."

"Drop it for *what*? —I know, I know. A horror movie. But you know something? Even if I wanted to make a horror movie, I couldn't. You know why? One very simple reason. I don't have a horror movie *script*!"

"*You* don't," Rick said, smiling slyly, "but *I* do."

*Goddamnit.*

*I walked right into it.*

*The pitch.*

*Fuck.*

"Four people," Rick began. "Father, mother—stepmother, actually—and two daughters."

"That would make four," Larry said, but Rick went on undaunted, impervious to irony or interruption.

"The father is stern, roughhewn, dignified—think Kris Kristofferson … it's dinner time. He's saying the prayer. The stepmother's head is bowed. So is the head of the older daughter. But the younger daughter's head isn't bowed and her eyes aren't closed. They're open—wide open. And what do you think she sees?"

Larry shrugged. "It's your story, not mine."

"She sees—and she's the only one who does—she sees a beautiful naked woman walk out of the kitchen, cross to the table, pick up the carving knife … and drive it into the base of the father's skull. Then the naked woman pulls the knife out, walks around the table and slits the stepmother's throat. Blood sprays across the white linen tablecloth. The naked woman wipes the blade on her breasts, then holds the knife out.

"Beth reaches for the knife, hesitates … Her fingers wrap themselves around the knife handle … Her eyes meet the eyes of the naked woman. 'That's right,' the naked woman says. 'Now—kill your sister.'

"' —Beth? … Beth?' A different voice is speaking now—it's her father. She looks up. The naked woman is gone. Her family is staring at her. It takes her a moment to realize that the prayer is over and they're waiting on her. 'Amen,' she says, 'amen … '

"Cut to Sunday morning. We follow Beth through the day. From home to church and back again. We see the family dynamic. The daughters get nothing, the stepmother gets everything. We see how the father caters to her, how she browbeats and condescends to her stepdaughters, and we watch the tension build. During the day, the daughters are able to maintain the façade, keep the resentment they feel under control. But at night … Night is *hell.*

"Beth thrashes about in bed, crucified by desire. She knows she shouldn't have those kinds of thoughts. But *they* say she should. *They* say it's all right. *They* want her to have those kinds of thoughts … "

Rick pointed at Larry's wineglass. "Do you think I could have a little of that? My throat's kinda dry."

Larry discovered, to his amazement, that he was leaning forward in his chair. He signaled to Carlo and waited with ill-concealed impatience as another glass was brought to the table and filled with wine. Rick took a sip and sighed appreciatively.

"Is this the house wine? If it is, it's awfully good."

"*Who* wants her to have those thoughts?" Larry said. "Who are *they*?"

Rick took another sip of wine, then set his glass down.

"The people who visit her dreams," he said. "The laughing cavalier. The Negro servant. The beautiful naked woman. They talk to her. They want things from her. They tell her what she should do. She won't listen to them—she *can't*—but they're wearing her down. It's getting harder and harder to refuse them.

"She knows that something is very wrong—that some line has been crossed forever—when she wakes up one morning—and sees the cavalier standing by the window. He doffs his hat to her, he smiles, and then he vanishes.

"And now the day becomes as terrible for her as night. Now she sees them when she's awake. The cavalier, moving through the house. The Negro servant, standing silently in the yard. The naked woman and the cavalier rutting in her parents' bed. She watches them go at it like animals ... She's disgusted, appalled and yet ... and yet ... It's too much for her. She faints.

"She wakes up in her room. She tries the door, but it's locked. She hears her father saying that he's sent for the doctor; she was found screaming in her parents' room, and he's locked her in for her own good. She sinks to the floor and weeps. And then—a hand touches her shoulder ...

"The cavalier stands there with a wicked smile on his face and a cat o'nine tails in his hand. He tears off her blouse and flogs her. The leather bites into her flesh. She loves it and she hates it. She wants it stop and she wants it to go on forever ...

"Her sister finds her half-naked and bleeding. She tends to her sister's wounds. She asks what's happened, and finally Beth tells her about the cavalier. And the older sister confesses something: she sees the cavalier, too. And the Negro servant. And the beautiful naked woman. They come to her every night, she says. She thinks she's losing her mind.

"And then the sisters tell each other everything: how they hate and fear their stepmother; how they believe she doesn't really love their father at all; how jealous she is and how she always works against them; how they have to settle for homemade dresses when she can have fancy clothes from Boston or New York. Above all, they talk about the visitors, the ghosts—whatever they are. And what they can do about them. If there's anything they can do at all … The doctor arrives. Beth and her sister tell him everything's fine, everything's all right.

"But things aren't right, not right at all. Dinner, with its knives and forks, is torment. Beth dreads being asked to bring in firewood—she could so easily crack her father's skull with one blow. She can almost picture it happening—brains and blood—and no! She couldn't do that. She *wouldn't*. She loves her father, even if he's too strict, too unbending. No—her, it'd be *her* head, her stepmother's. She doesn't love us and we don't love her. It'd be so easy to … *No!*

"She tries to force those thoughts away. But her visitors won't be quiet. They won't stop telling her what to do. They won't leave her alone.

"One morning the older sister almost kills the stepmother when an argument gets out of hand. The older sister knows just how close she came to actually committing murder. Beth finds her packing a valise and begs her not to go. I have to, says the older sister. I'm afraid of what might happen if I stay. And I'm afraid, Beth tells her, of what might happen if you leave. But she can't convince her, and her sister goes.

"Now she's alone in the house. It's just her, her parents, and her ghosts. And the real struggle begins. Day or night, they won't leave her alone. There's nowhere she can go that they don't appear. She can't keep those thoughts from her mind. She knows what her life is, what her life should be—she should be free. That's what they tell her. Free to live her life the way she's always dreamed of living it. Free to find pleasure. To find love. To be touched here, and here, and here …

"'Who's keeping you from that life?' says a voice. The beautiful naked woman sits on the edge of the bed. It's your stepmother. She doesn't love you. She's stealing your father's love. She drove your sister away. There's only one thing you can do. Kill her. As long as she's alive, no one will love you. Don't you see that? No one will ever love you … No one but me.

"The beautiful naked woman undresses Beth. Her body, uncorseted at last, trembles under the woman's hands, under the woman's lips.

"This is freedom, the woman says. This is what you've wanted all along—isn't it?

"Yes. No. Yes. She can't think. She has no time to think. Her stepmother will find out. Find out she's free. Find out—*everything.* And then she'll tell her father …

"It's then she realizes the truth. Freedom isn't desire. It's not the cause of freedom, it's only the result. How perfectly clear it's become to her. Freedom is something else.

"Freedom is an ax.

"The place is Fall River, Massachusetts. The year is 1892. She is Lizzie Borden."

Carlo appeared, refilled Rick's glass and then returned to his post, discreetly out of earshot.

" … So," Rick said. "What do you think? Any possibilities?"

"Maybe. Yeah. Some holes in it, but—"

"Don't give me that, Larry! It's fucking fantastic. It's a unique slant on an old story and it's perfect for today's market. There's sex, there's gore, and Lizzie's a great part for some hot young actress. You see what I'm talking about?"

"I'm sorry, Rick. It's just not my bag."

"Don't tell me you're going to let this slip past you."

"I'm committed to this thriller, Rick I can't walk away from it just like that."

"Sam would have. He knew when to take a chance."

"Well, you know something? My father's dead. I'm the one in the family who makes movies now. And I'm not interested in your Goddamn Lizzie Borden horror movie. In a thousand years I couldn't be less interested. Get it?"

"Larry, listen to me—"

"No! Jesus! … Are you *trying* to piss me off? … Okay, look—we both loved the old man, so I'll go this far for you. As a tribute to him, okay? … Give me the script and I'll see if I can get it to someone who'll look at it. Susan, maybe. But I'm not promising anything."

"I understand."

"Give me the script and then leave me the hell alone, all right? I've got work to do."

"Here's the thing, Larry … It might take a day or two."

"What's the hold up? You want me to give the script to Susan or not?"

"I do. Of course I do. The only thing is, uhhh … I haven't written it yet."

"What?"

"So it could take more like a week before I could get it to you."

"You don't have a script?"

"No."

"So what've you been telling me here?"

"I have the *concept*, Larry. The rest I was just … " Rick shrugged. " … Making up as I went along."

"Have you got a treatment?"

" … Not exactly."

"Is that a yes or a no?"

"Larry, I just had the concept this morning. But if you *want* a treatment—that I could give you in, oh … I could drop it by your office later today."

Larry pushed a napkin across the table. "Write your number on this and I'll call you when I've talked to Susan. If she's interested, we'll take it from there, okay?"

"That's great. That's super. Thank you. Sam would be proud of you, Larry."

Rick scribbled a number on the napkin.

The door to the street opened and a tanned, sharp-faced man in a silk shirt, ascot and blazer over gray flannel trousers entered and peered owlishly around the restaurant.

"Derek!" Larry called out. "Over here."

The man crossed to Larry's table. "Sorry I'm running late," he said in what might have been genuine old Etonian.

"*You're* sorry," Larry muttered.

Derek turned to Rick and gave him a toothy yellow smile. "I don't believe we've met."

"He was just going," Larry said.

"Rick Turnbull," Rick said, getting to his feet.

"Derek Mitford," the man said, and they shook hands. "Friend of Larry's, eh?"

"I've known him since he was a kid. In fact, I wrote a movie for his father once."

"Did you really?"

"*Trailer Park Tramps.*"

"Extraordinary," Derek said. "Lovely to meet you." He sat down and picked up the thriller script. He turned watery blue eyes toward Larry. "Have you finished it?"

"I loved it, Derek. *Loved* it. I've got a few questions, naturally—"

"Larry?" Rick said, hovering uneasily near the table.

"Naturally."

"Not so much questions, really, as observations."

"Larry?"

"You didn't think the ending was too … "

"Not at all."

"Larry? Sorry to interrupt, but … "

"The murder in the church isn't too … "

"*Larry.*"

"What?"

"You'll call me, right? After you talk with Susan?"

"Yeah, I'll call you."

"Fantastic. I think we're really onto something here, Larry. Nice to meet you, Derek."

Derek said something that might have constituted a response, or might not have.

Rick looked back once before he stepped out onto Las Palmas. Derek and Larry were already deep in conversation. He might have heard Larry saying something about the thriller being dead, but that was just one more thing he'd never be entirely sure of.

*** 

## AX ME AGAIN

… Wynman described the first film scheduled for production as a "radical revisioning of the Lizzie Borden story," with a screenplay penned by Derek (*Night Birds*) Mitford and Wynman himself. "Normally I'm just happy to serve as a producer," Wynman said. "But this project was … different. I had some very strong ideas about how the story should— how the story *must*—be shaped by and for modern sensibilities. The way I see it, Lizzie was not a monster. In a weird and awful kind of way, she struck out against the confining strictures of the times she lived in, when the options for women were far more limited than they are today. I see her as the first feminist, really."

—*Daily Variety*

\*\*\*

*If the old man could see me now …*

## AX AND IT SHALL BE GIVEN
## BORDEN PIC CHOPS UP WGA COMPETITION,
## AIMS FOR OSCAR

" … I believed in Fall River from the start," Wynman said. "At a time when the only movies that seem to make money are teen comedies or smash-and-crash CGI extravaganzas, the fact that our picture is out-grossing the competition proves that audiences are hungry for something different. The success of Fall River confirms my belief that the only key to success is a real story, well told. And call me crazy, but it all starts with the script." And speaking of scripts, does he think that he and fellow penman Mitford will take home the gold on Oscar night? "That's up to the Gods and the Academy. Just being nominated is a thrill."

*—Daily Variety*

\*\*\*

*… He wouldn't believe his Goddamn eyes.*

It was sometime after three in the morning, and Larry was feeling no pain: a blood test would have shown at least five different legal and illegal substances circulating through his veins at that moment. He had no doubt he could add another three or four before the night was through. He'd lost track of Derek somewhere along the Strip, but he hadn't lost track of a little golden naked man named Oscar. Oscar stood in a welter of champagne glasses and kept a mute watch over the waves of tuxedos and evening gowns that crested at Larry's table. He listened to the words of congratulations, witnessed the hearty bear-hugs and delicate air-kisses. If he saw the way the young woman's slim, golden-nailed hand moved along Larry's thigh and tended increasingly to linger around Larry's zipper, well … Success was a marvelous thing. The best aphrodisiac ever created. The best, the very, very, very best—

"—Larry," the young woman said, "you like it or not?"

"Sex?" he said. "I love it."

"*X*," the young woman said. "Not sex. *X*. You like it?"

"I love it," Larry said.

The young woman dropped a tablet into Larry's champagne glass. "Then drink up, sport."

Larry lifted the glass to his lips. "X marks the spot," he said, and drank.

\*\*\*

The exact sequence of events that followed wasn't clear to him.

He knew that he and the young woman had gone off in search of the limo, and that for some inexplicable reason they hadn't been able to find it. He remembered shouting and being shouted at, and then staggering backward and stumbling into a bus bench. So at some point he must have been outside. But now he was in a cab, and the cab was speeding along the freeway. But which freeway? And to what destination?

"Hey." Something nudged him in the ribs. "Hey."

He swiveled his head in the direction of the voice. It was like moving a concrete truck.

The young woman dug the golden-nailed toes of one bare foot into his ribs again.

"Larry, you awake?"

" … I'm breathing."

"That's always a good start."

Larry slumped against the seat. His head ached and his mouth was desert-dry. His mind sluggishly reviewed the events of the evening. It was all a blank from the time he arrived at the restaurant to this moment. " … Where are we? Where are we going?"

"My place."

"Where's that?"

"Don't worry. We're almost there."

A semi whipped past them with a shuddering sound. The gust of wind it left in its wake rocked the cab. The driver signaled and switched to an exit lane. The cab zipped up the ramp, slowed, and took a left. It rolled through a nondescript LA neighborhood, past the usual donut shops, beauty parlors, storefront churches, check-cashing places and liquor stores. Another left, then a right, and soon the businesses were replaced with dark hulking buildings and vacant lots. It could be Korea Town, Larry thought, or it might be … Truth to tell, he didn't have any idea where he was.

The cab stopped in the shadow of one of the buildings. The streetlights were out at this end of the block and the interior of the cab was in almost total darkness.

"We're here," the young woman said. "Pay the driver and we'll go in. Sixteen dollars and eighty cents, Larry."

He fumbled his wallet out of his hip pocket with difficulty. The movement made his head throb. His fingers felt clumsy, wooden.

The young woman tugged his arm. "Larry, hurry up."

"Just a minute. I just … I can't see a Goddamn thing in here." He leaned toward the driver. "Could you … "

The dome light went on.

Larry withdrew a twenty and a five from his wallet and shakily held them out. "Here you are. Just keep the change."

The driver turned around to take the money. Yellow dome light spilled across the pudgy, sweating face.

"Thanks, Larry," he said. "I appreciate it."

*Rick Turnbull. Goddamnit.*

"Could you help me get him in?" the young woman said. "The Larry-Bear is having a little difficulty walking."

*** 

Together they managed to get Larry out of the cab and into the building. They deposited him on a couch in the middle of a vast loft space filled with paint cans and tools and piles of 2-x-4s. Extension cords snaked across the rough wooden floor.

The young woman reappeared with drinks. Rick took his, but Larry shook his head numbly. "Come on, pal, drink up," Rick said. "Tonight's your night. You gotta celebrate, gotta live a little." He put the glass in Larry's hand. "*Skoal.*"

"Rick," Larry said, "I know how you must feel … about the … "

"The movie?"

"Yeah."

"You think I'm angry at you, huh? Pissed off? Enraged? Livid? Is that what you think?"

Larry nodded. It was too much work to speak.

"I was—once. In fact, I was furious, I'll admit it." He sat down beside Larry. "I even started drinking again. Can you believe that? But now … I'm over it now. You saw something good, and you took it. It may not have been right, it may not have been ethical, but that's the way the game is played. And you played it perfectly, all the way down the line." He patted Larry's knee. "Congratulations."

"I'm going to change into something more comfortable," the young woman said.

"You do that," Rick said. He watched her tugging off the red evening gown off as she left the room. Then he turned back to Larry. "Elsie's a beautiful young woman, isn't she?"

"Beautiful."

"I think she likes you. I've got a sense about these things." Rick set his drink on the planks-on-boxes that formed a crude coffee table. "Well. As I was saying … You handled it really well. When you knew I didn't have a script, a treatment—anything—you just walked in and stole my idea. By the time I got wise to what was going on, which was the thing in *Variety*, it was too late for me to do anything. It'd look like I was ripping you off instead of the other way around. You had me. Sam'd be proud of you, Larry. He made a whole career out of ripping off the powerless, and you're following in his footsteps."

"He never," Larry said.

"You know what I made off *Trailer Park Tramps*? 2500 bucks. 2500 total. That's all. And the film made millions. Sam screwed me over so bad I could've killed him. I could have murdered that bastard. That cheap-ass son-of-a-bitch bastard you called Daddy."

Larry struggled to his feet. "You can't talk about Sam that way."

Rick stood up. "He was a prick, Larry. And so are you."

He bent over to get his drink for a refill, and that's when Larry swung at him. The blow glanced ineffectually off Rick's shoulder. Rick straightened up. He smiled sadly.

"A prick—*and* a coward," he said, and slammed a fist into Larry's face.

*** 

Larry came to as Rick cranked the winch and Larry was hoisted into the air by the padded handcuffs around his wrists. The young woman—wearing nothing but a plastic see-through apron—knelt at Larry's feet and snapped on the ankle cuffs attached to rings in the floor. Then she stepped out of Larry's line of vision, and a moment later he heard a motor whine and the sound of metal grinding on stone. Rick began slicing off Larry's clothes with a carpet knife. Larry tried to cry out, but the ball-gag reduced his efforts to a muffled gurgling.

"I couldn't find a pair of scissors," Rick explained. "The place is a mess now, but when it's finished it's going to be one of the best dungeons in LA."

"*The* best," the young woman said over the grinding noise.

Rick tore away what was left of Larry's tuxedo pants and tossed them onto the shredded jacket and ruffled shirt. He walked out of sight, returning a moment later with his scuffed leather jacket on and a bag in one hand. He pulled the mouth of the bag open, revealing Oscar's bald golden pate.

"I'll keep an eye on this for you, Larry. I like to think I had a little something to do with it, you know?"

The grinding noise stopped. Rick turned to the young woman.

"You take good care of Larry, now. He's a mover and a shaker and he only deserves the best."

The young woman moved into Larry's line of vision. Light glinted off the silvery edge of the freshly-honed ax she carried. Larry began to shake and twist violently.

"I'll take care of him," the young woman said.

Rick zipped up his coat on the way to the door. "So, Rick—call me, okay? Let's do lunch or something."

The young woman started toward Larry.

Rick opened the door. "See ya later, Elsie."

"Rick!" the young woman said. "You know I hate it when you call me that."

"It's your name, isn't it?"

"I know that, but I *hate* it. Elsie, Elizabeth, Beth … I hate 'em all."

"Then what should I call you?"

"What everyone does," the young woman said. "Call me Lizzie."

Rick bowed elaborately. "Then good night, fair Lizzie, and may all your dreams be pleasant ones."

The young woman giggled. "You're crazy."

Rick put a finger to his lips. "*Shhhh.* I know I am," he whispered. "But don't tell anyone, okay?"

Rick closed the door behind him, walked through the loft and out to his cab.

\*\*\*

Driving away, he briefly considered checking in with the dispatcher, but changed his mind. He'd stay off duty for the rest of the day, then pick it up again in the evening. Or maybe even the next morning. Right now he wanted a drink, a bath, and some sleep. He was tired, so very tired …

The sun was just peeking over the foothills when he reached his apartment building.

# Echo Park, 1949
## by Joseph Goodrich

Awake at last he finds the room has subtly altered,
And his body—arms and legs—an eternity away.

He rises slowly, starts toward the window, hesitates.
He turns to face the bed, the chair, the ticking clock.

Nothing's changed,
But still the apprehension something's gone.

His genuine cowhide wallet?
The pocket comb missing a few blue teeth?
A cigarette or two from the open pack
Next to the picture of home on the dresser?
Or is it something else?
Something that he …
No.

He lights a Lucky—not a cough in a carload—
And crosses to the window.

Whatever it was,
They can keep it.
Whatever it was,
Whatever the hell it was …

He pulls aside the water-stained velour,
Then lets it sag again against the flaking wall—

And stuffs the battered gladstone quickly.
Of the essence, always, Time:

No time to wonder now
Who's waiting on the street below,
No time to wonder now
Who's coming this way down the hall,
No time at all to wonder now
Whose knuckles rap the plywood door.

# The Curlew Affair
## (for Ross Macdonald)
## by Joseph Goodrich

As I came into the lobby and got my key
Once again I made a loop in my life

(One of the stranger mysteries
But satisfactory in all its beautiful
Broken-down strangeness)

We sat at a big oval table
Poised at the intersection of something
Like every car in Paris

He was perfectly charming
Extraordinarily human and humble
In a gray suit, gray tie
But the strain was beginning to show

Several years back
I saw them in the supermarket
Her attitude was wonderful
The answer of course was yes

She was madly in love with him
It must have been the week
Before Christmas

We were talking
She was always talking

I really think
She was talking
With foolish joy

But every sound was a threat
Every word a kind of warning

You will understand me when I say
She died young
And nothing short of historic

"Do you think you can help me?"

I said yes
As the waiter cleared the table
Yes as always
One way or another
It's all one case

And I am so prone to getting lost

# Casual Encounter
## by Jake Hinkson

THE CRAIGSLIST THING STARTED innocently. At that time, I was working as the tech writer for a company that designs educational software, and I needed something to do in my spare time. Like every other bored, stumbling-toward-middle-age married white guy, I decided I would learn to play the guitar. I went on Craigslist to find a cheap one, but then I drifted over to the "Men Seeking Women" section. Just to see what it was like. I rooted around in there for a few days, and then I took the leap into the section for "Casual Encounters."

It was crazy place to be (and it felt like being in a *place* rather than just sitting on the couch looking at a screen). It was, simply put, a place where people were hunting for sex. Even if you figured that 99% of the posts were bullshit, that still left 1% of an endless ocean of indecency. And it was so raw. People weren't coy. They wanted to fuck in the park at night. They wanted to cheat on their spouses. Women wanted to fuck in the broom closet at work, in public places during business hours, in restrooms at random gas stations. Some didn't care what you looked like. Some wanted fat guys.

I figured I'd post an ad on a lark. What the hell. It was all in fun. I'd never actually do … *it*. And I really, seriously thought I never would. How could I? Meet a stranger for sex? I'd only had sex with two people in my life. I'd post the ad just to get off on the thrill of doing it.

And it worked. Just posting the damn thing sent a cocaine jolt through my body:

*Guy in his twenties looking for a high school or college girl for sexy fun times. Let's get crazy.*

I felt like an idiot writing it. Sounds idiotic. Hell, it is idiotic. But that's how people talk on there. That kind of asinine language is shorthand for *I'm dead serious about this. I'm not trying to be charming. Contact me if you want to get fucked.*

A few days passed. Nothing happened. I actually got really depressed about that for a day. I'd check in every five minutes and … nothing. I couldn't even get an anonymous stranger to flirt with me on the Internet. What kind of loser fails at that?

And I didn't need the rejection right then. My marriage was barely functioning after my wife had had an affair the previous year. She was a shift manager at Barnes & Noble, and the dude she'd fucked was a waiter at a Mexican restaurant in the same strip mall. They went to a motel and put it on our credit card. Since she usually paid that bill, she thought I'd never see it. The motel made a mistake, though, and charged her three times for the same visit. Computer error. That same afternoon I was going through the drive-thru at KFC without any cash and had to use my card. When it was declined, I called Visa and some bored call center operator in Bangladesh told me, in so many words, that my wife was banging someone on her lunch breaks.

We'd gotten through that—by which I mean the guy dumped her and she stayed with me—and I tried not to hold it against her. I mean, if I could have banged a waitress at a motel, I'm sure I would have. I'd stayed faithful because I didn't have any other choice.

But then a girl named Traci wrote me back on Craigslist and asked what I was up to.

My stomach dropped. I wrote back and said, *Nothing. What about you?*

And that's how it began. It went on for days. She was interested. She'd had sex like this before, and she loved it. Nothing serious. Just some fun. She asked how big my dick was. She said she could meet me. Then she said she was fifteen.

When I read those words some distant door slammed shut. I was alone, but my face started burning like the whole world was watching me. I wasn't sure how I got there. To be honest and up front with her, I told Traci I was thirty-two. I asked if that was cool. She said it was. The last guy was forty, she said. She liked older guys.

I debated it. It was crazy. But, she'd had experience. Maybe even more than me. Plus, all the kids are doing it these days, right?

We decided to meet the next day. My wife would be at work. Perfect. I'd pick Traci up, and we'd find a place. After I Google Mapped the nearest park that night, I could barely sleep. At midnight, I had diarrhea. For the rest of the night, I just stared at shadows on the ceiling and listened to my wife's acid reflux. The next morning, I got up, locked the bathroom door and jerked off. I thought that would diminish the desire to go meet Traci, but it didn't.

After my wife left for work, I took a shower. I clipped my nose hairs and my fingernails. I put on clean clothes and splashed on some cologne that was a seven-year-old Christmas present from my mother-in-law. Then I drove over to the park. I rode in silence. I've never been as scared of anything in my life as I was that first time.

I rode around the park. Every girl seemed to be Traci. She was a brunette with brown eyes. I saw a half-dozen girls who fit the description, but she said she'd be wearing a green skirt and a red tank-top. No Traci. I drove around for an hour. No Traci. I got out. Walked around. I got back in my car and went home.

Her message was waiting for me. She'd chickened out.

I told her I thought she wanted this.

*You've done this before, right?*

*yes*

*You don't have to do it. You know that.*

*i know but i want to. Its just im nervous.*

*But you did it before.*

*i was nervous then to*

After a while, we agreed to meet. This time, she'd meet me at the motel.

*** 

The next day I wasn't as scared. You can't build up the same rush again. I was anxious, but my nerves had been shot the day before. I didn't jerk off this time, either.

As I was leaving, my wife was sitting at the kitchen table, staring at her laptop. I told her I was going to go to the mall and see if Gamestop had the new whatever.

She didn't look up from the screen. "I might call you later to tell you to pick up some stuff at the grocery store," she said. She double clicked on something. "Make sure you leave your phone on."

"Why would I have it off?"

"What?"

"Why would I turn my phone off?"

She frowned at the screen and clicked on something. "Just make sure you leave it on," she said.

I said okay and left.

I zipped through the city streets. I sped the whole way. I caught every yellow light. I got there at noon. I'd check in, text her, and Traci would show up ten minutes later.

At the front, an elderly Asian man in a Superman t-shirt was working the counter. He took my card. Since my wife's affair, I'd been in charge of the credit cards. Karma's a bitch.

The old man took down my information. He gave me a key attached to a piece of plastic with a faded number 27 on it.

I walked outside, around to room 27 and unlocked the door. There was the bed. I texted Traci: *Room 27. Come and get me.*

\*\*\*

The cop who arrested me was an attractive black woman with a square jaw and bemused eyes. Her name was Trenita Ohakim. I remember it from the trial. O-ha-kim. She handcuffed me while two other cops—both men—looked on, smirking. They did not take their job seriously. Or maybe they just thought I was the butt of a joke.

I wanted to cry, but I couldn't. I couldn't even feel enough at that moment to cry. I said, "May I go to the bathroom?"

"You'll have to wait," Officer Ohakim said.

"I can't," I said. "Really. I think I'll piss on the seat of your car."

She uncuffed me and one of the other cops led me to the bathroom and stared at me while I unzipped my pants and took out my pathetic dick. We stood there in silence.

"Want me to turn on some water?" he asked.

"Sure."

Behind me, water splashed against the sink.

\*\*\*

They put me in the back of Officer Ohakim's car. The seat was hot and smelled like old plastic.

As she drove, I said, "I wasn't looking for underage girls."

She didn't say anything for a while. I wasn't sure she heard me.

When we stopped at a light, she leaned to her right as if she was looking at something in the seat beside her. She said, "You specified high school girls."

The light turned green.

I looked down at my clothes. Jeans fresh out of the laundry. A red button-up shirt. I had picked them out because I thought Traci would find me attractive in them.

My face burned.

"Were you the one writing the posts?" I asked Officer Ohakim.

"Yes."

I looked out the window. We were turning down my street.

"Wait, why are we here?" I asked her. I broke out in a sweat. "Oh Jesus. Please don't do this." Tears surged to my eyes, but I held them back. "Please, officer."

"We have to seize you computer," she said. "Is your wife still at home?"

They knew I was married. Of course they did. This was happening. There was no warning. This was happening now.

I started to cry. Not hard. Not sobbing. But there was no sucking it in. "Yes," I sputtered.

We stopped and one of the cops in the car behind us walked up to Officer Ohakim's window. He asked her, "Is his wife at home?"

"Yeah."

He left and walked up the path to the door of our apartment and knocked. I looked away when the door opened.

After a moment, Officer Ohakim said, "She wants to see your face, sir."

I turned. My wife was standing in our apartment doorway looking around the officer. When she saw me, she put her hand to her mouth and started crying. He had to help her steady herself against the doorframe. She looked fat and pathetic and stupid. I know, because I caused her to look that way. She had been sitting at the kitchen table looking like a regular person, and then a police officer knocked on her door and told her that her husband was under arrest for soliciting sex from a minor. I'd only been gone from the house about thirty-five minutes.

He followed her inside. A few minutes later, he came back outside carrying my laptop. My wife came to the door and looked at me. She put her hand to her mouth just as she had before, just as if it was happening all over again.

\*\*\*

I was convicted, but I got released early after thirteen months. First time offender. Crowded jails. My lawyer argued that I was an idiot but not a monster and added that I'd already lost my wife and my job when the story hit the papers. The judge gave me an ass-chewing and told me to get out of his face and make damn sure I never came back. I'm on parole for five years, and I have to register as a sex offender everywhere I live for basically the rest of my life.

Because I can't reside within six hundred feet of anywhere kids play or go to school, I live out on the edge of the city. I sleep in a lean-to under an underpass and my only neighbors are two weepy child-molesters and an eighty-year-old man who did sixty years in prison for multiple rape charges.

Now that I have no friends, I spend my days talking to myself in my lean-to, obsessing over everything that fell apart. I don't know how accurate my memory is anymore, though. I've thought about it so much, it's like a picture that's faded and crumbling at the edges.

When I can work, I do day labor. Lately, I've been doing this job, sitting in this booth at a car lot. It's a sweltering little box. The boss doesn't allow us to watch TV or read on the clock. So I sit here and sweat for eight hours. It's not hard work. In fact, it isn't really work. Work would at least feel like something. This is just an endless nothing. I sit here and sweat and wait for nothing.

Two days ago, near the end of my shift, I was sitting here sweating when I saw Officer Ohakim. She was with a guy. They pulled into my lot and parked and walked out past my box on their way to the restaurant next door. The guy was a handsome man with amber skin and a shaved head. He wore a suit. Officer Ohakim wore a navy blue dress. Looked like a first date to me.

As they walked past me, the man was laughing and saying, "I am for sure Roxy never said any such thing about you."

Officer Ohakim giggled. "Well, you are for sure wrong."

The man glanced at me and nodded. I nodded back. Officer Ohakim looked at me, smiled politely, and then when my face clicked for her, she stopped smiling. She stared down at her toenails. They were painted bright blue. She and the man walked to the sidewalk, and waiting for the light to turn, far enough away that I could not hear, she leaned over and told him the only thing about me that anyone remembers anymore.

# One-Step's Last Meal
## by Paul Krueger

### I.

THE WARDEN WAS THE sort of big man only Texas seemed to produce, and he could barely contain his glee as the guards hauled One-Step Grimes into his office and sat him down. He could remember when the notorious "last outlaw" had first come to the prison. He'd been wiry then, his black hair just giving way to grey. But while he'd fattened up some during his stretch inside, something still marked One-Step as a man to watch.

"Now, I'm guessin' you know what this is about," the warden said.

One-Step nodded. He pointed with cuffed hands toward a box on the warden's desk. "Mind if I have a smoke first?"

The warden nodded, giving One-Step a cigarette from the box. A guard lit it for him.

"Word came in this morning," the warden said. "Your number's up."

One-Step nodded again. "When?"

"Friday," said the warden. "You'll have the week to write your last statement, if you got one to make."

"I do."

"And then there's the matter of your last meal." The warden leaned forward. "We'll be serving it Wednesday."

"Thought I was being executed Friday. Y'all have to wait longer'n two days if you want me to starve to death."

"We give it a few days before cause we find a man starin' Hell in the face tends to lose his appetite."

One-Step shook his head. "I'll be hungry. Give it to me Thursday."

The warden slid over his ashtray. "Traditional meal's the Ted Bundy special: steak with fried eggs, hash, coffee, juice, and buttered toast," he said. "But lucky for you, we take requests. You'll get a day to think on yours."

"No need," said One-Step. "Been thinking on this for a while now. What I want is a cold six-pack and a big pot of chili to eat with it."

"That'll be fine," said the warden. "Any specifics?"

"Yeah. For the beer, something dark and strong and bitter. And for the chili … well, warden, I'd like to prepare my own last meal if that's alright with you."

"It's not," said the warden. "I ain't letting you anywhere near knives or anything like that."

"Well, warden, seeing it's my very last meal, I figured we could make an exception," said One-Step. "I even got my own recipe for it. Grimes family secret."

"Your last name ain't Grimes."

One-Step smirked. "Look here." He turned in his seat to one of the guards. "What's your name, son?"

"Chandler," said the guard.

"You cook much, Mr. Chandler?"

"Some."

"I'll let Mr. Chandler here cook my last meal for me," One-Step said. "I'll supervise. Pains me to give up my secret recipe, but it beats going to Judgment without that chili on my lips." He stabbed out his cigarette.

The warden weighed his options. "You got any problems with this, Mr. Chandler?"

"No, sir," said Chandler. "Be a good story. The last meal of the last outlaw."

"Reckon it would," the warden said. "Well, alright then. I'll run it past the board, but I think we got us a deal." He offered his hand. One-Step took it and shook it. "Mr. Chandler, stay here a sec. Mr. MacDonald, you take One-Step here back to his cell."

One-Step got to his feet. "Come by me when you're done. I'll have a shopping list set for you." And as MacDonald carted him off, he smiled.

***

One-Step Grimes was named One-Step Grimes because when he'd been roaming free, he'd always been one step ahead of everyone after him. No one knew where the last name Grimes came from; it wasn't his, but it fit anyway.

But One-Step's name was hardly the only mystery about him. In fact, when it came right down it, everyone knew a whole lot about what he'd done, but no one really knew much of anything about who he was.

There were no matches to his fingerprints, or his teeth, or even his DNA, and he had no medical record on file. He had no known family, and all his friends knew about as much as the Fed. No one even knew where he came from. The Texas drawl that made his words drip so lazily was flawlessly authentic, but so was the Boston whine he spoke when he was up there, or his Wisconsin warble. The best people could figure, he was from America, and even then some weren't too sure.

After an eight-year spree of thefts, murders, and arsons across twelve states and a stretch of Mexico, One-Step had been cornered in an old Texas ranch house, all out of steps to take. The County Sheriffs found him lounging in the living room with expensive bourbon and a cheap cigar. He'd stared down their guns as he drained his glass, then taken one last pull of smoke giving himself up.

The whole time, he'd never stopped smiling.

He refused a lawyer, while all his old enemies were loaning the government the nastiest ones they could afford. Now that he was caught and caged, everyone wanted a piece of One-Step, the last outlaw. But on day one of the proceedings, One-Step pleaded guilty to every single crime he was accused of. He'd been inside ever since, marking his time. It didn't seem to bother him any.

"You want something, you can always take it," he'd often say, "but it's a lot easier if they just give it to you." He wouldn't give a damn who heard him say it.

*** 

When Chandler came by the block, One-Step slid the shopping list to him through his cell bars. Reading it over, most of the ingredients made sense. A few were head-scratchers, though.

"Of course, venison," One-Step said. "It's leaner'n beef."

"Don't think you'll have to worry about your heart," said Chandler. "But alright … beer?"

"Most folks use water. I like flavor."

Fair enough, Chandler figured. But one item on the list really stood out. "Peanut butter?"

One-Step grinned. "The Grimes family secret. Thickens the sauce, cuts the acid. And best of all, blends great with the paprika. Far as my chili goes, it's the MVP."

"Never heard of no peanut butter in chili," Chandler said. "Don't seem like the two would go together."

One-Step shrugged. "It's my last meal. Any other questions?"

Chandler shook his head.

"Then I'll see you in a few days." He thought a moment. "Hey, Mr. Chandler. You think if I ask, they'd give me a Viking funeral? Burning boat and everything?"

Chandler snorted. "One-Step, when you're gone, the only reason folks'll bother to mark your grave at all's so they know where to piss."

One-Step considered this. "Yeah," he said, then laid down in his bed.

Chandler brought the list straight to the warden as instructed, and the two men pored over it. They couldn't find anything out of place. It was ridiculous, they told themselves, to think that a pot of chili could save a dead man.

But this was One-Step Grimes. Most men passing through the prison walls gave themselves nicknames and spent their time trying to live up to them. One-Step's was given to him and well-deserved.

## II.

On Monday, Deputy Lenny Elmore of the US Marshals came to visit One-Step. Of One-Step's enemies, Elmore had been his most persistent and successful. He'd tracked One-Step everywhere, sometimes missing him by minutes. It'd been a long chase, but also the most rewarding one of Elmore's career. He'd been the one to finally corner One-Step in that ranch house, and when they'd busted that door he'd been the first one inside.

He was already waiting in the visitor's room when One-Step was brought in. "Hello, One-Step," he said through the glass. He spoke with the bland radio-news cadence of Illinois.

"Marshal," One-Step said. His Texas twang was gone. Now it sounded like he and Elmore could have grown up on the same street. Maybe they had. "I expected you sooner."

"You're not the only thing for me to chase," said Elmore. "But I took time off for this. I figured I owed it to you. I heard you made your last meal request."

"That's right."

"What's on the menu?"

"A six-pack of dark and bitter, and a pot of chili. My own recipe. One of the guards is cooking it for me."

"Sounds good," said Elmore. "One guy I read about requested a lump of dirt."

"Really?"

"Yeah. The request was denied, though. He had to settle for a yogurt."

"I don't see much difference."

Elmore laughed.

"So," One-Step said, "are you just here to get a good seat for the show?"

Elmore's mouth twisted. "Look," he said. "I want you to know I'm not here to enjoy this. I figured it'd be wrong if I wasn't there when you died."

One-Step could believe this. They'd been enemies, but when you were enemies with someone for that long, it made them something of a friend. "Thanks," said One-Step. "But while you're here, I've got a request."

Elmore raised an eyebrow. "Oh?"

"Yeah. Remember when I saved your life back in Kansas City? Since time's running short for you to pay me back, I figured you could do me one last favor." He hesitated. "I need you to find my father."

Elmore blinked, stunned.

One-Step grinned. "If anyone deserves to know some real truth about me, it's you," he said. "His name's Ray Digs Deep."

"'Digs Deep?'"

"He's one-fourth Arapaho. Not all of us get cool names with animals in them." He drummed his fingers on the countertop. "Find him. Tell him I'd like to share my last meal with him and make peace. And if you bring him here to do that, Marshal," he said, "I'll let you break bread with us. You find that man, you'll have earned it."

Elmore wrote everything down. "And who'll I say is asking for him? He surely didn't name you 'One-Step.'"

One-Step smirked. "He didn't name me anything. Doubt he'll know it, but if it helps, tell him it's from Leon. You've got until Thursday. Good luck." He rose. The Texas drawl returned as he called for the guard to bring him back to his cell.

***

The house listed as belonging to Ray Digs Deep was as run-down and out of the way as Elmore expected it to be. He parked his rental car down the road a ways so he could approach on foot. He got the feeling that a man like the one he supposed Ray Digs Deep to be would appreciate that.

After the first knock, Elmore heard shuffling feet inside, so he waited. When no one came to the door, Elmore knocked again, identifying himself as a US Marshal. He heard more shuffling, then several locks being undone before the door opened.

Elmore knew at a glance that the man glaring at him behind the screen door was Ray Digs Deep. When he asked the man his name, it was a formality. "I'm here because of your son, Mr. Digs Deep."

"Nice try," said Ray, making to shut the door. "Owen's long dead."

"Not Owen," Elmore said. "I'm here for Leon."

Ray paused. "Leon?"

"Couvier. Mother was a Jane Couvier."

"Not ringing any bells," Ray said. "But I had some wild days when I was younger. Might've left behind a little guy or two." This wasn't playing out the way Elmore expected it to. That troubled him.

"May I come inside, Mr. Digs Deep?" he said. "It'll only be for a second."

Elmore didn't judge the house too harshly from the mess inside. There were piles of clutter everywhere, but Elmore could tell that Ray was the kind of man who'd know exactly what pile to look in if he needed something. There was a strange system at work that Elmore could see, but not quite understand.

They sat down in Ray's living room, beers in hand. "I don't know if you know much about your son ... " said Elmore.

"I don't know anything," said Ray. "Don't even know if he's my son."

"He asked for you by name, and you're a guy that keeps a very low profile. Especially since you're protected as a member of the Arapaho tribe. If he hadn't known your full name, I wouldn't have found you at all. Besides, I've known your son a long time. Trust me, the resemblance is there."

"Alright, alright," said Ray. "What's he want with me? I got no money."

"It wouldn't do him any good," Elmore said. "He's on death row."

Ray nearly spat out his beer. "Jesus!"

"In Texas. His last meal's on Thursday. He wants to share it with you. He said he wants to make peace. I'm here to collect you."

Ray regarded him. "I have to go with you?"

"You don't have to," Elmore said. "But Leon Couvier's got another name. One-Step Grimes."

"'The last outlaw.'" Ray sneered. "That supposed to persuade me?"

"You've got a chance to look into the mind of a man who had American law enforcement eating out of his hand for nearly a decade. A chance he's never offered anyone else."

"I don't want a place in the history books."

"What do you want, then?"

"To ask you the same thing. You're some fed, and I'm an old Injun you're trying to invite to my bastard's dinner party. What's your angle?"

Elmore couldn't help but grin. There was that sharp mind he recognized. "I was the one who caught him. He told me if I brought you around, I'd get to join you both."

Ray laughed: softly at first, then louder until it was a booming cackle. "That's good," he said. "You want in on the Last Supper. Well, that's moving and all, but I don't owe anything to a son I've never met. Especially if he's bad enough that they're trying to put him down."

"I think you do," Elmore said. "Maybe he'd have turned out differently if you'd been there. One son dead, another one about to join him. Isn't it time you acted like a father?"

Ray's face hardened. "Don't tell me anything about being a father," he said. "You know as much as I do. I can tell by lookin'. If you got other business with me, get on with it. Otherwise, finish your beer and get out."

Elmore laid his card on the table, next to his drink. "I'm staying in town," he said, getting up. "I'm leaving tomorrow night at six. If you change your mind."

***

After Elmore left, Ray finished his beer, finished Elmore's beer, then got into his truck and drove to Spillane's on the edge of town. The usual crowd greeted him like a brother. He ordered some cheap scotch with one ice cube, like he always did. Halfway through it, he started telling everyone about the chat he'd had that day with the feds.

"That's a hell of a thing," said Dewey, the bartender. "Who knew you had it in you to make the modern-day Dillinger?"

Ray shrugged.

"You gonna go?"

"Why should I?" said Ray. "Either he rages at me for not being there, which I don't have much stomach for, or he gets all weird and religious on me, which I also don't have much stomach for. Besides, no point in reconnecting with a son that's got one foot in the grave."

"Or one step," said Dewey. The others laughed, except Ray. "You should go. He's family."

Ray lit a cigarette. The law didn't allow that, but Dewey, who was on his fifth smoke of the evening, didn't pay it much mind. Neither did anyone else. "I've got a hellbound son—who might not be my son—and a deranged fed trying to fly me down to Texas so he can watch us have a tea party before it's too late."

"It's One-Step Grimes," said Dewey. "*The* One-Step Grimes. You're telling me you're not the least bit curious?"

The others all chimed in too, and pretty soon Ray could see it was him against the rest of Spillane's. He finished his scotch and had another as everyone sent advice his way.

By the time he'd reached the bottom of his third glass, he'd made up his mind.

### III.

On Wednesday, One-Step and Chandler went to the kitchen. Per One-Step's instructions, the chili had to be cooked and then let to sit for a day before it was served to anyone. Under watchful eyes, he inspected every ingredient. When everything was to his satisfaction, the two set to work.

First, the vegetables: onions, green peppers, jalapeños, some garlic, and a different way for each one to be cut. On the whole, One-Step was patient but precise. As he liked to point out, it was his last meal; he wanted it done right. "Now, 'done right' means me doing it myself," he said, "but you'll have to do the best you can."

After that, the venison. The recipe called for ground and diced, a pound of each. The ground was easy, but sure enough, One-Step had a specific size for the cubed, too. "They call it dicing for a reason," he said, his fingers indicating an invisible die.

The whole way, Chandler kept a straight face, even though One-Step was starting to grate on him. After all, he was still a guard. If he'd wanted to, he could've artfully rearranged One-Step's bone structure with his nightstick, and that bloody mess and a room full of witnesses wouldn't have been enough to get Chandler in hot water over it.

"Sorry if I'm being hard on you, son." One-Step's voice snapped him back to the grimy kitchen. "It's rough, knowing how to do something easy as blinking, and then having to take it apart and explain it bit by bit to someone else."

"Sure, One-Step." Chandler was almost done with the venison.

"Now toss that in the pot with some oil, and while it's browning, we'll measure out the spices."

Chandler wasn't sure if the recipe was really that tricky, or if One-Step's way of instructing him was what made it that way. He'd be about to do something once, twice, and each time One-Step would correct him until he did it right. After the venison was browned, Chandler poured in the tomatoes (canned and diced), the vinegar, half the spices, and a few other things, and then they let it all simmer for an hour.

While the red mess inside the pot roiled and bubbled, they talked. Chandler kept his guard up at first, but bit by bit he let it slide as One-Step told stories of his time traveling the States, of all the strange folks he'd met. Probably by necessity, One-Step was a very good storyteller. So good, in fact, that he made it easy for Chandler to almost forget that the spaces between all these tales were the times One-Step was out doing the things that landed him on death row in the first place.

A few guards watched the two from a respectable distance, and Chandler kept a close eye on One-Step, but it was for nothing. One-Step kept his hands to himself, and not a scrap of supply went missing from the kitchen counter. Before long, the hour of simmering time was up, and One-Step went back to barking out orders. Under his guidance, Chandler mixed in the other spices and the beans.

"Real Texas chili don't have beans," Chandler said.

"This ain't real Texas chili," said One-Step. "It's Grimes chili. Peanut butter."

Chandler gave the peanut butter a sidelong look before scraping it into the pot.

One-Step nodded, satisfied. "Stir it well, son."

A minute later, the warden dropped in. "Hello, Mr. Chandler," he said. "One-Step. Just here to see how everything's going."

"Going fine, warden," said One-Step. "But could you do me a favor and look at me instead of the pot?"

The warden bristled. "One-Step, if you weren't getting pure death mainlined through your arm in a couple days, I'd have you beaten with a fire hose for talkin' that way."

"Sorry, warden," said One-Step. "I just don't want more folks knowing my secret recipe than necessary."

"I don't give a damn about your secret recipe."

"Sure you do. It's why you're down here." One-Step grinned. "I'm stuck in a cell all day, but I ain't deaf. Folks think I'm down here creating some kind of crazy chili bomb, or what have you."

"Just people talking, is all. Don't you go believing your own press."

"I don't," said One-Step. "They got it all wrong. I ain't trying to explode anything. I'm making me a batch of chili so hot it'll just melt the bars, and I can walk on out." When the warden didn't laugh, he sighed. "Look, fine. Inspect it if you want, but it's your boy's been making it for me this whole time. I'm a killer and a thief and a runner. I ain't a mad scientist."

The warden brushed past One-Step and stuck his nose over the bubbling pot. What filled his nostrils was spicy and hearty, jolting his system like a black coffee. "Smells good, Mr. Chandler," he said. "Not sure about those beans, though."

"Beans weren't my idea, sir." When the warden was satisfied that One-Step hadn't tried anything he made to go, but One-Step stopped him.

"Before you go," he said, "I wanted your permission. Mind if I finish off that beer there?" He nodded to the bottle of beer on the counter. The recipe only called for half of it, and the rest was just sitting there.

The warden shrugged. "Mr. Chandler, pour that beer there into a plastic cup and give it to One-Step here." One-Step accepted the cup gratefully, and the warden left.

Chandler dumped the vegetables into the pot. "I don't get why it mattered how they were cut," he said. "They're gonna give the same flavor either way, right?"

"Mr. Chandler, you're doing this thing the way I would've done it," he said. "Everything I do, I do for a reason."

"You got caught, didn't you?" said Chandler.

One-Step sipped his beer. "Guess I did."

## IV.

One-Step was quiet all Thursday. The guards outside his cell told the warden that nothing had changed too much. One-Step made his usual polite conversation, then busied himself with the crossword book an admirer had sent him a few months back.

But the warden wasn't fooled. One-Step wasn't going for a deathbed conversion or anything, but even a cool customer like him couldn't look Hell in the eye and shrug it off. And sure enough, when he walked by One-Step's cell, he saw One-Step frantically filling out puzzles, as though afraid he wouldn't be able to finish them all.

At five that evening, he was led from his cell to a bleak white interrogation room and took his place at the table that had been set up. The sides were already set, as were the toppings. An ice bucket sat at the table's foot, six bottles of dark and bitter nestled inside.

The chili was absent. One-Step had requested it be served later.

After two minutes, the door opened again. Two men came through: Deputy Elmore and Ray Digs Deep.

One-Step rose when they entered. "Thank you, Marshal," he said. They shook hands. He turned to Ray. "And you ... well." He offered his hand. "Leon Couvier."

Ray's heart sank. The smile, the calm greeting. This one was gonna get wackadoo religious on him, he just knew it. He shook One-Step's hand, forcing a thin smile. "Hi."

"Please, sit," said One-Step, taking his seat. The others followed suit. "I gotta hand it to you, Marshal, you were always able to do things I never could. Finding my dad ... you've definitely earned your place at this table." He handed them each a beer and took one himself. "You know, the whole time I was on my rampage, I was looking for you, old man. Came close, but never could find you. But the Marshal here, I give him a name and he brings you around in two days." He cracked open his beer and toasted Elmore. The other two didn't drink theirs.

"Where's the grub?" said Ray.

"It'll be coming in a second ... dad," said One-Step.

Ray shifted in his seat. He didn't like the way this one was calling him 'dad.' Owen called him that, and Owen was dead and buried.

"First, I just wanted to know what you remembered about my mom."
"Your mom?"
"Jane Couvier. Hammett, Missouri," One-Step said.

Elmore leaned forward in his seat. Another mystery solved.

"Sorry, kid," said Ray. "The list of broads in my life's as long as my leg, and the writing's real small."

"Fair enough," One-Step said, shrugging. He nodded to the one-way glass window. The door opened, and Chandler entered with a big steaming pot. The scent filled the whole room. "Gentlemen, this is Mr. Chandler here. He cooked dinner under my guidance. Pull up a chair, Mr. Chandler. You've earned a spot, too."

Chandler ladled some chili into each bowl, then some for himself. One-Step passed him a beer. The others dug into the sides, but One-Step kept his neat, with only beer to keep his bowl company. "Alright." He grinned. "Dig in."

They did. Its flavor was rich and heavy, the steam warming their faces as they ate.

"Not bad," said Elmore, swigging his beer. "I'm impressed, One-Step." One-Step nodded in thanks. He sweated and smiled at Ray, who after his initial reluctance now shoveled chili into his mouth.

But as he ate, Ray felt a tightness around his collar. He thought it was just the spice at first, but soon he sputtered like a broken engine and clawed at his shirt.

Elmore stood up so quickly his chair fell over. Seeing that Chandler wasn't choking, he pointed to the struggling Ray. "Take care of him!" Chandler sprang to obey as Elmore rounded on One-Step, shaking him by the shoulders. "What did you do?"

But he saw One-Step's blue face, heard the hollow breaths trying to escape his inflamed throat. He recognized the symptoms. "Anaphylactic shock," he said. He turned to Chandler, pointing at the chili. "You! What's in this?"

"Um," Chandler said, mind lurching. "Deer. Peppers. Beer. Tomatoes. Beans. Peanut butter. Jalap—" But Elmore wasn't listening anymore. He turned back to face the rapidly fading One-Step.

"Peanut butter," Elmore said. "You son-of-a-bitch."

*\*\*\**

Behind the observation glass, the warden and MacDonald watched. "Radio the medics," said the warden.

"Sir," said MacDonald, "they'll never make it."

"Record has to show we tried to do something." The warden didn't take his eyes off the scene unfolding inside the interrogation room. "You're right, though."

MacDonald raised his walkie to his mouth with a crackle.

## V.

Deputy Elmore stalked down the corridor to what had been One-Step's cell, still numb from the interrogation room. It'd been two hours, but at last they'd sorted out the red tape and the bodies were on their way to the morgue. He hadn't bothered going with them. He had one last thing to see.

He slotted his borrowed key into the cell's lock. The door slid open with a low groan that set his teeth on edge. He wondered how One-Step had felt, having to hear it at least twice every day. Had he gotten used to it? Or had it just become a daily habit of his to grit his teeth and wait for his spine to stop tingling?

The inside was tidy, for the most part. Marks and scratches covered the walls, but they looked old enough that Elmore could tell they weren't One-Step's. It was already like he'd never been there at all.

Elmore saw one trace, though: a crossword book under the pillow, every puzzle perfectly filled out. The last one was mostly blank, though, except for two words in spaces where they didn't belong:

THANKS MARSHAL

Elmore laid One-Step's final statement back on the bed, then sat next to it. He'd let the warden know about this, but first he needed a moment to process that in their decade-long game, One-Step had finally won.

And Elmore had won it for him.

\*\*\*

The warden quashed all news on the circumstances of One-Step's death. The press got more and more curious as to why there was no official statement, but the warden refused to indulge them. "I shut up long enough," he said, "they'll get bored and go away."

He was right.

Elmore departed Texas the following week, accompanying the body of Ray Digs Deep to Colorado. He gave his supervisors his report, but refused to talk about it with anybody else. After a few months he was more or less back to his old self, but every time he started to get cocky again he'd remember his time in Texas and get very quiet.

An inquiry was made into what responsibility Chandler could have held in the murder-suicide of One-Step and Ray. Ultimately, he was cleared, but the damage was done. Aside from the jokes about his killer cooking, he knew everyone saw him differently now. One-Step was gone, but his ghost lingered, and it haunted Chandler.

\*\*\*

Two years later, on a weekend when the kids were out of the house, Chandler went to the store with a long list. When he got home, he set about tossing all his ingredients into a pot. He tried his hardest to remember how he'd done it before, with that voice guiding his hand.

The three and a half hours of cooking time passed in silence, with a growing forest of empty bottles on his table for company.

That Sunday, he microwaved some: plain, with only a beer. The way *he'd* had it.

It was still the best he'd ever tasted.

# Hidden Dance
## by BV Lawson

She is old inside her grieving,
life dissolved in mascara tears,
dark and wet on a faded canvas
wrapped around her distances
where hidden bruises lie,
and lies become the paint of living
in violence of laughter
muffling screams at night,
when his hand falls the hardest;
The children cry their dreams,
flinching at the crack of thunder
in the other place, the chamber
where demons dance
and prayers of childhood
flutter to the ground,
flutter, to scatter and to cool.

# Waiting
## by BV Lawson

On a bench you sit alone and wait
for nothing more than waiting,
fusing with the peeling paint and rain.

Rages, sorrows, cross your cheeks,
each a line unto its own
like jagged streaks on shattered glass,

While strangers, passing through your gaze
withdraw into their coats and collars
turned against the damp and chill.

This is where the felons fly,
set free from bars to roost in shadow,
sentenced to obscurity,

Where deep in your world the night has fallen
leaving you to prowl your dreams,
all calluses and numbed embraces.

# Sometimes the Devil
## by Daniel Moses Luft

"NOTHING TO EAT HERE at all?"

"Sorry, I usually come home from the restaurant and fall asleep in front of the TV. Never keep much here besides breakfast and booze."

"Good thing I like your booze, David."

Natasha smiled as she leaned out of bed to root around in her bag for something. She was two inches taller than me without her heels and I could tell she worked out. She'd showed up at my Harvard Square restaurant with her East European accent, her long, black hair, her navy blue business suit, and her little suitcase rolling along behind her. She was in Boston for the night after her meeting and didn't need to be back to the airport until tomorrow afternoon.

"I can order out if you're hungry."

"What?" She looked up from her bag, a little startled. "No, no food. I will be fine. Perhaps another drink."

Then we heard the noise.

Her hand stopped in the bag as she looked up at me with wide eyes and an open mouth.

Someone was at the front door with a key.

"I think you better get dressed," I said as I slipped back into my shorts.

Before I was even halfway down the short hall to the living room I saw another woman in front of me. Joni looked tinier and blonder than ever after the hours I'd just spent with Natasha. She was wearing her yellow slicker, skinny jeans and duck boots. Some of her hair was matted against her face from the rain.

"Davy, I can't sleep," she said." I haven't slept for days and I'm just going out of my mind." Her slight frame brushed past me and her shoes squeaked on the hardwood floor. She was dripping wet.

"Umm, It's really okay, babe," I mumbled as I wrapped my arm around her and walked her back past the kitchen to the front door.

"I just hated the way it went last month. Why should I really be mad at the way you acted. I mean, my whole family is a bunch of losers and why do I care what they think. I don't even see them that often or you would've met them earlier. I just—I just miss you, Davy. I've been so lonely. We've been together so long and I ... " She trailed off as she looked at me then spoke in a lower tone. "You've been drinking."

I tried to smile but we were past the galley kitchen and in the living room where the couch and coffee table were, where two empty glasses sat on the table. She moved so fast she slipped a bit on her way to pick up one of the glasses.

"Lipstick?"

"Umm, well."

She didn't say anything, just threw the glass at me. I flinched when it shattered against the marble kitchen counter behind me.

"What the fuck, Davy? One fight and you've got some whore in bed with you? Is she already moved in?"

"No, it's not like that."

"Then what is it? I stopped at the restaurant but they said you'd left. I walked all the way here trying to think of the right thing to say so you wouldn't be mad at me anymore. I dressed in my tightest jeans because I know you love them and I just got rained on for half an hour while I was trying to convince myself to actually come up here, swallow my pride and make up with you."

I didn't know what to say. I just hoped Natasha had walked out the back door to the apartment or had hidden under my bed.

"Where is she? Where the fuck is she?" Joni was screaming, high pitched. Thank God the walls are supposed to be soundproofed.

"Who is this?" I heard the voice and the accent over my shoulder. Natasha was walking in behind me. I turned as I saw that she still wasn't dressed, just bra and panties.

"My god, look at the size of that fat bitch."

"She's not fat."

That was a dumb thing to say. Joni balled up her sharp, little fist and smacked me on the nose. I closed my eyes and she rushed by me.

She ran after Natasha and the larger woman was caught off guard; the only thing that kept her standing was that she was probably twice the size of Joni. I tried to put myself between them but it was a struggle. I'd block Joni and she would turn and go around me. I finally yanked her off Natasha and tossed her further than I thought I could. She went flying backwards and hit the back of her head on the shiny granite countertop. After that she fell to the ground and didn't make a sound.

Natasha slowly kneeled over Joni, reached down, and looked for a pulse. She tried the wrist first, then tried the throat.

"David, I don't feel anything. This woman, she has no pulse. She is not breathing."

I walked over to Joni and felt shivering cold. I tried to give mouth-to-mouth but her head and neck felt messed up. When I pulled my hand out from under her it was covered with blood. A red puddle expanded slowly around her head like some hellish, red halo.

"Oh, shit," I said as I backed away on my knees.

"She's dead, David," Natasha mumbled.

"What the fu …" I couldn't even finish. I just stared at her in silence.

"What to do now?" I heard from above me.

"Well, yeah. What to do now? I mean this was an accident. This wasn't supposed to happen. I didn't know she'd come back here. I didn't know she'd freak out. I mean she was really trying to hurt you, wasn't she? I mean she was always a little crazy jealous but she was the one who dumped me. She walked in on us uninvited."

"Well I guess you've got yourself in a little bind here, David."

Natasha's voice had changed.

All at once.

It still had an accent to my ears but Eastern Europe was all gone and now she sounded very local, raised in Massachusetts.

"What just happened?"

"What do you mean?"

"What are you doing? Why are you talking like that? Who are you?" I looked up from Joni into Natasha's eyes.

"Well, lets say, for the sake of argument, that I can help you with this."

"Help how?"

She smirked as much to herself as to me, the same as when I asked her back to my apartment. This time she didn't lean in to kiss me. This time she turned on her bare heel and disappeared into my bedroom. I watched that large frame and muscular legs as they didn't make a whisper on the floor.

When she returned she was still only half dressed in her blouse and slip. She was carrying the suitcase that had previously rolled behind her. She reached inside and pulled out a blue, legal-pad-sized, plastic envelope held together by snaps. She tossed it at me.

"Open it."

I did. There was more blue plastic inside.

"What is this?"

"Take it out, unfold it. It's pretty strong. Could probably hold two of her."

"We should call the cops."

"The cops? Do you want them here?"

"They need to know."

"That you killed her?"

"It was an accident."

"Looks pretty nasty to me. Your old girlfriend walks in on you while you've got me tipsy and in bed and you kill her in an argument when she interrupts us."

"It wasn't like that. Joni was out of control. She could've done anything."

"Like kill you? You've got fifty pounds on her. Kill me? I'm twice her size and in twice her shape. Either one of us could've picked her up and gently carried her back outside the building. Could she have picked you up and thrown you onto that marble kitchen counter, David? Davy?"

I didn't answer.

"Nope, this was murder or at least manslaughter."

"It was an accident."

"Anyone know she was here?"

"Probably not. She lived alone."

Natasha placed her warm, dry hand on my cold, clammy shoulder. "Do yourself a favor, David. Unfold the plastic."

I looked down at Joni, the puddle around her head had stopped growing. It was just a little gash back there but it bled out a foot around her head.

"This will work for both of us. And everything is going to go great for you if you do as I say. Now take the plastic out of the bag."

I pulled it out of the blue envelope and began to unfold it onto the floor.

"It's big. It'll hold her," she said. Her tone was softer, more helpful. "Maybe get a towel and clean up the puddle before you put the plastic closer to her. Get some from the kitchen."

I grabbed two towels and came back. Natasha was pouring herself another drink. I mopped up the blood and tossed them onto the sheet.

"Now pick her up and put her in the middle."

I leaned over and picked her up like I used to when I carried her to bed. I laid her gently on the middle of the sheet.

"Nice going, now you have to throw out your shorts."

I looked down and saw the blood on my underwear.

"Maybe you should've just rolled her. Anyway, toss 'em on her and wrap her up."

I took off my underwear and placed them next to her, then I rolled both sides around her and Joni disappeared inside the tarp.

"Hey David, you're not rolling a yoga mat. Fold it over at her head and feet. You don't want anything showing or dripping."

It took a minute but I got it done. It looked tiny, hard to believe Joni was even in there.

"Got any packing tape? Duct tape?"

"I think so, in the bedroom closet."

"Let's both go in there and get dressed too." She patted me on the rear.

We walked back together. I didn't want to look at Natasha. I didn't want to hear her speak. I didn't want her to see me naked again. I didn't want her in my apartment. But when I was dressed and tying my shoes I did look at her again.

"Hey, who are you?"

"Me? I'm just some easy girl you picked up at your restaurant. You got me very drunk and drove me here in your nice Jag. We had sex in this room and then I saw you kill your ex-girlfriend in the living room."

She smiled and walked out of the room with her heels in her hand.

"So why did you come here?" I called down the hall.

"Just get the tape, David; don't ask too many questions." She turned and looked at me over her shoulder. "Let me say this. If you do what I say you will watch the sunrise in a couple hours from this very living room. If you try to fuck with me or even just do less than I tell you, you're going to spend a lot of time in jail and that's the only place you'll see the sunrise for a long, long time. You get me?"

I wanted to throw up and fall asleep at the same time as we re-entered the living room.

"I get you."

"Good. Now tell me a few things."

"What?"

"First lift that end."

I picked up Joni's feet and Natasha began to wrap the duct tape around the bundle.

"This girl."

"Joni."

"Fine, Joni. Is she rich?"

"What? No."

I was lifting parts of Joni off the floor while Natasha wrapped the tape around her.

"Is she related to anyone rich?"

"Not that she ever told me about."

"What did she do?"

"What?"

"For a living, what did she do?"

"She's an office manager. Was an office manager, lately she's been temping."

"And does she have much family?"

"Some, but not here, mostly in Cincinnati."

"Does she drive a car?"

"No, just takes trains and cabs mostly."

"This one's really important. Did she ever have a government job? Even a little one like working in a courthouse snack bar? Was she ever a teacher, even a substitute?"

"No, never. Why?"

"Ever committed a crime? Was there ever a reason for her to be fingerprinted?"

"Shit no."

She nodded. "All good."

The blue plastic wrap around Joni now had a spiral of silver duct tape around it.

"Now what?" I asked.

"Now we get her out of here really, really quietly because the guy who lives at the bottom of the stairs is really, really nosey."

I cocked me head and she actually smiled at me

"I'll open the door. You have your keys?"

"Yeah. Where are we going?"

"Where do you think? Some place where we can get rid of her." She looked at me as if I were some stupid kid.

"You don't need me to help you carry her do you?"

"I don't know."

"Well try to figure it out. Get her over your shoulder."

I leaned down and picked Joni up by the sides of the plastic. I'd carried her many times before but this time 1 almost dropped her. Natasha reached out to balance Joni on my shoulder then she re-taped a bit of the tarp that had come open.

"I guess I'm ready."

"I don't want any talk in the hall and I really don't want to help you carry it."

"No. I've got it."

"Good, I'm parked very close."

"You're parked here?"

"Just shut up for now. Come with me and do what I say and you're going to be okay."

I frowned and nodded.

"Don't make a sound on the stairs. Who knows if we're gonna run in to anybody inside or on the sidewalk." She pulled a small pistol out of the black bag. It looked like one of those semi-automatic things.

We eased out the door and down the stairs. Her eyes were everywhere looking at the doors, up the stairs behind us, and onto the sidewalk outside of the glass door on the first floor. She looked ready to leap or shoot at anyone including me. I followed behind like her hunchbacked assistant. I took each step slowly, aware of every slight crack or pop from the stair as I placed my foot on it. Each sound bounced off the walls in the hallway like cap gun shots.

She shushed me as we passed by the nosy guy's apartment but nothing happened. She opened the door and I felt the rush of August humidity as I stepped outside. The rain had reduced to a drizzle.

I saw a flash of headlights as she pressed the fob to unlock her car. It was a grey sedan with a small, fiberglass boat attached to the roof. She popped another button and the back trunk opened. She didn't say anything and simply waited for me to slide Joni off my shoulder into the trunk. I did it and she snapped the trunk shut as the two of us looked up and down the street for any sign of movement.

"Get in," she said as she walked to the driver's side.

We drove in silence through a few lights. I spoke first.

"Pretty big trunk in this car."

She laughed to herself.

"Yeah, you know, the Sonata gets a bad rap as a cheap car, I guess all Hyundais do, but I like it. It's easy to steer and parallel park, gets decent mileage and, yes, it has a huge trunk."

"Yeah."

"Hell, we could've put two of her back there."

"How long have you had it?"

"It's not mine."

We headed out of Cambridge and into Arlington. Arlington was a very different kind of town that liked to pretend it was a faraway suburb instead of part of Boston. There was no one on the street and most of the houses were dark. We passed a police cruiser that had lights on but the officer inside was asleep behind the wheel.

"So what about the accent?"

"What about it?"

"Why did you use it and where did it go?"

"Don't sweat the details, David. Maybe I got it from my grandparents or maybe I just liked Bullwinkle when I was a kid."

"Your name's not really Natasha, is it?"

"Does it really matter? This will be the second time tonight that I'm doing something really nice for you. Don't start with all the hows and whys."

She turned left at a church and we were on a dark side street for about a block. Then the road ended in a parking circle. It took my eyes a moment to adjust to the darkness and I realized we were next to water.

"This is the place." she said and got out like we were parking in front of her home.

I got out and saw that she was untying the boat from the top of the car.

"Untie the other side," she said. We had the boat off in no time and the two of us carried it to the edge of the water.

"Now we go get that thing."

"Where are we?" I whispered back as we walked back to the car.

"Spy Pond. You've never been here before? Not very deep but no swimming and no fishing—not allowed. Toxic chemicals. Really beautiful in the daytime though, you should come here."

She opened the back and left me to pick up Joni as she grabbed something heavy from a dark corner of the huge trunk. I walked to the boat first but I could hear her behind me. I laid the rolled-up tarp in the middle of the boat and looked over my shoulder. She placed a long coil of heavy rope and two anchors into the boat.

"So you know what we're going to do?"

"Yeah, I figured it out. Will this stuff hold it all down?"

"This will hold anyone down. It's Kevlar rope, water-resistant. It won't break and these anchors are way more than enough to sink it all for good."

She stepped into the boat and gestured for me to push it off. I pushed hard and the boat slid silently onto the water. I hopped in, stepped past her and over Joni before I sat down.

"You row," she said. "I'll tie the ropes and keep a lookout for cars and lights."

"Where do you want me to go?"

"Just out. Get away from the bank and I'll tell you when it's deep enough."

I rowed for a few minutes in silence. The boat moved quickly across the water. The rain had stopped while we were in the car and the crickets were out. It was a soothing sound. Part of me wanted to relax.

"Over there." She pointed past my shoulder. "Over there is the deepest part. That's where we're going."

"How do you know?"

"You want me to tell you to trust me again or do you want me to tell you to shut up? That's where we need to be."

I rowed a little more to my left until she told me to stop.

"Let's do this gently. No splash. With the two anchors it'll lay flat on the floor of the pond and we've got about thirty-six feet down there. No one will find it."

"That's not very deep."

"But remember, no swimming, no fishing. It's more than three stories of dark, muddy water that people sometimes kayak on. Never happen. This thing is gone."

Neither of us stood up. We did a combination of rolling Joni and shoving her over the side. She made almost no noise as my hands held onto her until she was under the water. The two of us stared off the side of the rowboat until the air bubbles from inside the plastic wrap dissipated then stopped entirely.

Joni was all gone.

"That's it. Now let's go back to your place."

I dipped the left oar into the water and turned the little boat around and headed toward the launch site where we had first entered the water only about fifteen minutes earlier. We tipped the boat back over the roof of the car and reattached the ropes very quickly until it was secure.

"Let's go." she said as she pulled the keys out of her pocket.

We drove back to my place without saying a word. After she parked I led the way back into my apartment building. It was starting to get light out. I unlocked the door and walked inside wondering why she wanted back in my apartment. I pulled a beer out of the fridge and looked at her.

"You work out a lot."

"Yes, I'd have no trouble carrying you down a flight of stairs if I really needed to."

"Since I'm not dead, could you please tell me who you are and what's going on?"

"Well, let's just say you've just had the luckiest night of your life."

"Why's that?"

She stood up and walked past me to the galley kitchen. When she came out from behind the counter she was holding my biggest, sharpest carving knife. I tensed as she approached me but she kept walking to the far side of the living room without looking at me.

"I used to have a boyfriend," she said as she turned around. "Not a husband, just a boyfriend. He was a contractor. Did drywall and nice wooden trim."

"So?"

"Do you know when this building was gut-rehabbed?"

"No idea."

"'Course you don't. It was a dump until it was sold two years ago. My guy worked on it but it didn't pay as much as he needed. So it wasn't his only job."

She turned away to dig the knife into the wall next to the window. Then she began to saw the blade in and out of the plaster. After she had carved a big square she pulled away broken pieces of plaster and paper. She reached into the wall and tried to pull something out but it was too big and she had to use the knife to cut away more drywall. Then she pulled out a dusty, white, plastic bag, a kitchen garbage bag folded over and taped shut with faded blue painter's tape.

"Money," she said as she held up the bag and walked closer to me. "That guy downstairs, the nosey little shit. He doesn't like anyone poking around the building when he's here and he's always here. Thank Christ he goes to bed by early."

"How long have you been watching me? What were you going to do to me?"

"David," she grabbed my jaw with her hand as if she might kiss me again. "I don't think there's any reason to hash out the details of anything that might've happened here but didn't."

She paused to make sure I didn't answer and the room was silent again.

"So who was that chick on the floor?"

"Up until a few weeks ago she was my girlfriend."

"Up until a few weeks ago I had a boyfriend."

"What happened to him?"

"Not much. He's still in Walpole. His partner killed a security guard when they were getting this money. The verdict came down last month. I could've waited for him to come out on the robbery charge but they were both convicted of the murder so he won't be getting out for at least another decade."

"So that's it then."

"He doesn't know it yet but, yeah. And now that I'm holding this I feel pretty good about it. I think the court did me a favor."

"Maybe yeah."

"And I just did you the biggest favor of your life. You had an accident that was definitely going to have you up on manslaughter charges at least. Now you're just a witness in a missing person case that may not start for a month or two."

"And you got what you wanted."

"Yes, but remember, I was going to get that anyway." She walked past me and tossed the knife in the sink. "I think you owe me something for the service I have provided."

135

"Provided?"

"Yes."

"What do you want?"

"No more than I was willing to risk losing here in the bag."

"What does that mean?"

"I want a hundred thousand dollars."

"What?" My eyes opened wide and I leaned forward. She stared back at me and I saw the gun was in her hand again.

"I think that's fair."

"I don't have that kind of money." I looked at the gun and tried to calm down.

"Well I'm sure you've got a personal bank account and an account for work that only you have access to. That restaurant you're managing is doing a nice business. Remember, I've been watching."

"But I can't come up with that much."

She stood up and looked taller than ever.

"How about this, I'll give you two weeks. I'm sure you can find a way to cook the books at the restaurant. Maybe apply for a loan. And I'm sure you can scale back in your personal life. You don't need to be driving that Jag, though it was fun to ride in it with you. You only live a mile from Harvard Square anyway. Maybe walk to work or get yourself a Sonata instead." She smiled at her own joke.

"I don't take home that much in a year."

"Yeah, but you need to find it now. Break your lease. What do you need with a big place like this when you practically live at work? For Christ's sake it's a crime scene. I wouldn't stay here if I were you."

"If I get it what do I do with the money."

"Oh, you're easy to find. I'll find you and you can give it to me. If you don't have it you'll never see me again. You'll never see anyone again."

"Why didn't you just kill me the minute you got inside my apartment?"

"As I said before. I just broke up with my guy and wanted a bit of fun first. And it's a good thing I didn't. That tiny, blonde chick would've let herself in while I was cleaning up. So it's all good for both of us, David, Davy." She leaned in and aggressively kissed me. I could feel the pistol against my head.

Then she turned around and let herself out of my apartment. She shut the door to the hallway and I heard her heels on the stairs. I heard the door downstairs open and shut and then I heard her heels out on the sidewalk as she returned to her car. She only idled the engine for a moment before she drove away.

# Bad Gun
## by Suzanne Lummis

Bad cause it's cheap, cheap and bad. *Saturday Night Special* they call
    it, *Trash Gun.* The slide. The bullet can get caught between the Now
    and the Split-
Second-Later, between the Here and the Hereafter. Hard. A thick, flat,
gun-shaped weight that gets harder in your hand when you close
your hand around it. *Raven,*

say the letters pressed on the barrel. *Raven Arms. GUNS* says the shop
    on Highland Boulevard. Bad cause she bought it and she wanted it
    and it
maybe wanted her. No questions asked. A hundred twenty bucks on
her Visa credit card. Cause someone might want to kill her
and she might not want to let them. You never

know. Might not suit her mood. Bad cause it slips into a bad hand. One
    day she puts her key in the lock but the door's already open. *Uh oh.*
    Drawers burst
and spilling, messier than usual—the wash-and-wear, well-worn articles
lie in their colors. Just a square empty space where the typewriter'd
been. Rug gone. Gun

flown. *Raven.* Well. Days and weeks. Two months. They go by. Along
    comes
a police, one police. Knock knock. He sits in the deep, discount store,
    chive
colored chair that came with the place: Single apartment circa 1928,
kitchen that she'd paint heartbreak red, alcove, built-in dresser

with drawers that open

for a thief. In a plastic bag he holds a small cheap gun. Registered to
   her. Safe, sound. A nice police, quiet, he looks at her with a quiet
   gaze. Bad gun—
man pointed it at his wife in a domestic dispute. That's what he
calls it, a "domestic dispute". It's not legal to point a gun
in a domestic dispute. It's

not polite. She signs a paper and he leaves the thing with her. First
   she was not
a gun owner, then she was, then she wasn't—now she is again. *Hmm.*
   Like a
fish-slippery bird it slid toward a wrong hand, now it's back. What
   kind
of hands are hers? *Hmm.* Bad gun because it made her forget
to think, bad because it made her forget

to ask. It's a bad gun because she forgot to think to ask, *Did he pull
   the trigger?*

# Wonder Woman, Private Eye
## by Suzanne Lummis

"Beautiful as Aphrodite, wise as Athena,
strong as Hercules, swift as … " etcetera …
O.K., it's Hermes, in case you've forgotten—
little winged lad, pretty boy, transmitting
his messages door to door, dispensing
his favors. I'm done with all that,
with the myth racket.
Even the land of the Amazons,
that tribal thing, for me—like the kids say—
it's *so over*. Now, I work alone.
I go one foot softly over the other,
flightless, low
as the humans, and moving as they do,
over asphalt. It happened like this.
One night, as I hurried through atmosphere
(just *half* the speed of light, and I was late),
in my tall shapely boots, and whatever leg-
bearing one-piece job DC had me sporting
that year, I caught a touch
of ennui, disgust actually, and self-disgust.
Suddenly, I wanted the Truth.
I wanted all the terrifying, many-headed
forms of it, which made my twinkling"lasso of truth" look like
   Tinkerbell's dainty
little wand. Then came
the call of the wild, pull of the dark—deep
and knowing. I was sick of cartoons.

You ask (the boys ask—always,
they want to know), so what am I wearing?
Not a trench coat (cliché), a jacket, cinched
at the waist, leather, color of tarnished silver,
many black- zippered pockets, outside
and in, jeans like a normal woman—and, yes,
I'm licensed to carry. Heat.
Now get your mind off my body and on
this one over here, soiled by daylight,
jammed under a dumpster
on Alameda, south of the old train yards.
Seems most of his blood
escaped through the same hole.
Sure, I'll call 911, speed-dial the LAPD.
But I'll be working my own angle:
who is the real culprit?
The jackass who pulled the trigger,
or the deadbeat, no-show dad,
or the dull, ignorant mother,
the neighborhood that gave up, city
that turned its back, world that was busy
elsewhere? Space
in its icy beauty, rushing toward
no place, discharged from nothing?
Who, where, *what* is *The Arch Villain*?
Hmm …

I wonder.

# Kept in the Dark
## by Charles Rammelkamp

"Look, Mom doesn't need to know
Ronnie was murdered last week.
She's just had a stroke.
The news will kill her."

"But Ronnie was her nephew,
her sister Edith's son!
She needs to know."
Pleading with my older sister,
my voice hits a high whine.

"Why? Mom wasn't even close to Ronnie.
Edith's already dead,
and Mom hasn't spoken to Howard
since Edith divorced him, what,
twenty-five years ago?
There's no reason
we should tell Mom."

I see my sister's point,
but it just seems wrong,
all that not-knowing.

# The Silent Scream
## by Charles Rammelkamp

Mrs. Penrose next door told reporters
the burns on my face were "unreal"
where Mama pushed lit cigarettes
into my cheeks and lips.
But they were real, and yes,
my mama did make me eat my shit
and drink my own piss,
when I was a kid,
and then she'd hug me to her, fierce,
and tell me she loved me.

So I don't know
if I wouldn't have raped Mary Lou
if I'd had a different childhood.
But I did rape her,
And I sure as hell
would have killed her again
or she'd have squealed on me so loud
I wouldn't even be able to hear
my mama's voice in my head.

# My Dolls Hate Chicken Nuggets
## by Stephen D. Rogers

My daddy is a pornographer
Taking nude photos of girls my age
Posed in lewd positions
A recession-proof business that
Puts a roof over our heads
Food on the table
And toys in my room

Momma takes me out when daddy is working
So I won't make friends
And I finish all my food despite
The smell of sweet and sour

# On Furlough
## by John Ryan

The thought of it was better than the actual furlough.
Two days before release, his delirium
could have been mistaken for lock jaw,
the way he hummed tight-lipped, smiled all sugar.
He had scraped and saved like the worst skinflint
and his ribs bulged like a ship's curving futtocks.

That's what he yelled at the revelers, "Futtocks,"
a nautically mysterious word, that first day of furlough.
People who dared called him worse than skinflint
but he couldn't hear them in the carnival delirium:
Barkers and bare bulbs, and all the spun sugar
he sucked to the last till it pained his tight jaw.

And what would they see if he opened his jaw?
How it pointed, prow-like, the worn teeth set like futtocks;
the rot of alcohol and refined sugar;
the tongue a captain, whipping out orders for furlough;
the lips a bow wave, plunging into delirium;
the whole ravaged enterprise, the work of a skinflint.

Well? He kept his gold hidden, remarkable skinflint,
and rubbed at the beard like seaweed on his jaw.
If he kept his eyes open he'd part the delirium
like the scissoring buccaneer ride creaking on its futtocks.
There was only one promise to a day of furlough:
he would let his lips part for a taste of *that* sugar.

When he mounted up the Spook House, she said, "Hey, Sugar."
He parted with his bills with the look of the skinflint.
She asked, "How many days 's it you're on furlough?"
He held up one finger; she began to stroke his jaw.
Her back got all bruised on the little boat's futtocks.
The darkness of the tunnel sucked away the delirium.

The last ghost overhead signaled vanished delirium.
He sucked on his teeth having lost all the sugar;
she smoothed her dress's ruffles like a series of futtocks
and smiling with just her mouth said, "Don't be such a skinflint."
He worked around some words that didn't make it past his jaw
and passed her the rest of his money for furlough.

His head began to swim like the delirium of too much sugar.
Setting his jaw for the long, empty night of the skinflint,
he rocked on ribs like sodden futtocks, beached on a bench till the
    end of his furlough.

# A Definition of Noir
## by Gerald So

eluded me
as smoke writhes
from a recent-left
cigarette,
a dab of lipstick
the last clue
whose it was,
until we met
and I oh-so-slowly
learned what it was
to want you,
love you, hate you,
forgive you,
with no hope
it meant
a damned thing.

# Who's Who

## Authors

**James Campbell** attended the Institute of American Indian Arts in Santa Fe, where he studied painting with Fritz Scholder and also attended the occasional writing workshop with N. Scott Momaday. Living today in the old mining town of Bisbee, Arizona, he often consults on the state of the universe with a cat named Happy Hour. He's recently been following James Crumley's advice to "get it written down," and with some encouragement from fellow noir enthusiast and former publisher Dennis McMillan, along with novelist Kent Harrington, he's making progress on an autobiography.

**Bill Crider** is the author of more than fifty published novels and numerous short stories. He won the Anthony Award for best first mystery novel in 1987 for *Too Late to Die*. He and his wife, Judy, won the best short story Anthony in 2002 for their story "Chocolate Moose." His story "Cranked" from *Damn Near Dead* won the Derringer Award and was also nominated for an Edgar® and an Anthony Award. He's also won the Golden Duck Award for best juvenile science fiction novel and been nominated for a Shamus for *Dead on the Island*. His latest novel is *Half in Love with Artful Death*.

**www.billcrider.com**
**www.billcrider.blogspot.com**

**Thomas A. Crowell, Esq.** is a mouthpiece for dames and palookas looking to sell their dreams to Tinsel Town. He started off as a writer and producer for kid's television, creating the award-winning *Professor Potto's Videolabs*, before turning to the dark side and becoming a lawyer. He counsels clients on a wide range of entertainment law and intellectual property rights issues: from film and television, to comic book publishing, music, and the graphic arts. He is the series editor of the Focal Press *Pocket Lawyer for ...* series, and author of both *The Pocket Lawyer for Filmmakers* and *The Pocket Lawyer for Comic Book Creators*.

**www.thomascrowell.com**

**M. Dante**'s Black Dahlia Creative began in New York City in the early 1990s as interactive performance art and role-play with a modern noir and slightly surreal mystical theme. She is also associated with The Philadelphia Erotic Literary Salon, now celebrating six years of success in Philadelphia. Her work has been published by *The Erotic Literary Salon*, *Slixa Late Night*, *SenSexual* and *Headpress UK*. Her image has most recently been transformed by artist Steven Johnson Leyba as part of his "Sexgoblin PooRtrait" series, and can be seen in archive on the websites of New York photographers such as Fred Hatt and Efrain Gonzales.

**Richard Godwin** is the author of critically acclaimed novels *Apostle Rising*, *Mr. Glamour* and *One Lost Summer*. He is also a published poet and a produced playwright. His stories have been published in over thirty-four anthologies, among them his anthology of stories, *Piquant: Tales of the Mustard Man*. His fourth novel, *Noir City*, will be published in 2014 in English and Italian by Atlantis. Godwin was born in London and obtained a BA and MA in English and American Literature from King's College London, where he also lectured.

**www.richardgodwin.net**

**Joseph Goodrich** is the author of the Edgar® Award-winning play *Panic*, editor of *Blood Relations: The Selected Letters of Ellery Queen, 1947–1950,* and a frequent contributor to *Mystery Scene*. His fiction has appeared in two MWA anthologies. A former Calderwood Fellow at the MacDowell Colony, he lives in New York City.

**Jake Hinkson** is the author of the novel *Hell on Church Street* and the novellas *The Posthumous Man* and *Saint Homicide*. Hinkson is a regular contributor to *Noir City, Mystery Scene,* and Macmillan's website *Criminal Element*. He has written for *The Los Angeles Review of Books, Mental Floss,* and *Bright Lights Film Journal*. His books *Hell on Church Street* and *The Posthumous Man* are being translated into French by èditions Gallmeister and will be released in Europe in new hardcover editions in 2015. His newest novel, available from Beat to a Pulp, is *The Big Ugly*.

**www.jakehinkson.com**
**www.thenighteditor.blogspot.com**

**Paul Krueger** is a Chicagoan-turned-Brooklynite-turned-Angeleno. He likes cooking, karaoke, carpentry, comic books, and other hobbies that start with fricatives. His first novel, currently untitled, is due out next year from Quirk Books. Twitter is his great vice (@regularpuke), but perhaps his biggest flaw is that he never finishes what he

**BV Lawson**, poet, author, and journalist, grew up in rural East Tennessee, where she won a poetry competition at the age of ten. After earning two degrees in music, she continued her passion for creative endeavors by writing feature articles and fiction for dozens of national publications. A three-time Derringer Award finalist and 2012 winner, BV was also honored by the American Independent Writers and Maryland Writers Association for her Scott Drayco series. BV currently lives in Arlington, Virginia, with her husband and enjoys flying above the Chesapeake Bay in a little Cessna.

**www.bvlawson.com**

**Daniel Moses Luft** lives in Somerville, MA, with his wife and four small-but-fast kids. He's had fiction published in the *Best New England Crime Stories 2012* and *2013* as well as *Out of the Gutter, Spinetingler* and *Beat to a Pulp*. He has reviewed books for mostlyfiction.com, *The Violent World of Parker*, and *Mystery Scene*. He's been a substitute teacher, a bartender and traveled with three circuses. He also dragged his wife to Moscow for their honeymoon.

**Suzanne Lummis** is a poet whose work has appeared or are forthcoming in *Miramar, Solo Novo, Hotel Amerika*, in the special "Noir Issue" of the Australian magazine *Contrappasso*, and *The New Yorker*. In 2011, her organization The Los Angeles Poetry Festival produced a twenty-five-event, citywide series "Night and the City: L.A. Noir in Poetry, Fiction and Film." Her essay, "The Poem Noir— Too Dark to Be Depressed," was published in *Malpais Review*.

**Charles Rammelkamp**'s most recent book is *Fusen Bakudan*, published by Time Being Books, a poetry collection involving missionaries in a leper colony in Vietnam during the war. He also edits an online literary journal called *The Potomac*. Finishing Line Press will publish his poetry chapbook, *Mixed Signals*, later this year.

**Stephen D. Rogers** is a multi-published writer of fiction, non-fiction, and poetry. Over eight hundred of his stories and poems have been selected to appear in more than three hundred publications, earning among other honors two "Best of Soft SF" winners, two Derringers (with seven additional finalists), a Shamus Award nomination, a Rhysling nomination, two "Notable Online Stories" from story South's Million Writers Award, honorable mention in "The Year's Best Fantasy and Horror," mention in "The Best American Mystery Stories," and numerous Readers's Choice awards.

**John Ryan**'s short stories have appeared online in Akashic Books' "Mondays Are Murder" series, *Shotgun Honey, Out of the Gutter, Suspense Magazine*, and *MARGIN: Exploring Modern Magical Realism*. His poetry has appeared in various print magazines, including *River Styx*. His collaborative story "Hothouse by the River," which introduced private detective Ed Darvis, was produced in a limited letter-press edition at the University of Iowa School for the Book. He is currently looking for a publisher for his first novel featuring Ed Darvis, *Allegiance Under the Skin*.

**Gerald So** edits *The 5-2 Crime Poetry Weekly* at poemsoncrime. blogspot.com. His own poetry has appeared recently in *Beat to a Pulp* and Silver Birch Press's *Noir Erasure Poetry Anthology*. Follow him on Twitter @g_so

# Judges

**Jay A. Gertzman** is the author of *Samuel Roth, Infamous Modernist* (University Press of Florida) and *Bookleggers and Smuthounds: The Trade in Erotica, 1920–40* (University of Penn Press). His article on Stanley Kubrick's *The Killing* has appeared in *Cashiers du Cinemart*. He is currently researching the poet/novelist Michael Perkins, and preparing a book-length study of David Goodis.

**Allan Guthrie** is the Scottish author of several noir crime novels, including the Edgar-nominated *Kiss Her Goodbye* and Theakston's Old Peculier Crime Novel of the Year Award-winner *Two-Way Split*. When he's not writing, he's a literary agent with Jenny Brown Associates and co-founder of digital publisher, Blasted Heath. His most recent novel is *Slammer*.

**Woody Haut** was raised in Pasadena but now lives in London. He's the author of *Pulp Culture: Hardboiled Fiction and the Cold War, Neon Noir: Contemporary American Crime Fiction, Heartbreak and Vine: the Fate of Hardboiled Writers in Hollywood*, and a novel, *Cry for a Nickel, Die for a Dime*, published by Concord Press.

**www.woodyhaut.blogspot.com**

**Vicki Hendricks** is the author of *Miami Purity, Iguana Love, Voluntary Madness, Sky Blues*, and *Cruel Poetry* (a finalist for an Edgar Award in 2008). Her short stories are collected in *Florida Gothic Stories*. Love of animals and nature, apparent in her earlier novels, comes to the forefront in her recent novel *Fur People*.

**www.vickihendricks.com**

**Andrew Kevorkian** can best be described as a "communicator." Currently, he is a public-relations consultant and a writer and editor, and has been, over the years, a journalist and an adjunct professor of both journalism and public relations, on the college level in both Philadelphia and London, where he lived and worked for twenty-eight years.

**Edward G. Pettit** is a Philadelphia writer, professor, book reviewer, film presenter, public lecturer and all around literary provocateur. He is known as the Philly Poe Guy, but also recently served as the Charles Dickens Ambassador for the Free Library of Philadelphia's yearlong Bicentenary celebration of the author's birth in 2012 and wrote the Ebenezer Maxwell Mansion's 2013 murder mystery play, *Twisted*, in which he played Dickens.

**Dennis Tafoya** is the author of three novels, *Dope Thief, The Wolves of Fairmount Park*, and *The Poor Boy's Game*. His short stories have appeared in anthologies including *Philadelphia Noir* and *Best American Mystery Stories*.

**www.dennistafoya.com**

## Editors

**Lou Boxer** is co-chair of NoirCon along with Deen Kogan. He is a life long bibliophile addicted to great writing and the human condition. He supports his avocation through his full time vocation as a physician.

**Cullen Gallagher** is a writer and musician living in Brooklyn, NY. His work has appeared in *Beat to a Pulp, Bright Lights Film Journal, Brooklyn Rail, Crime Factory, Hammer to Nail, Los Angeles Review of Books, Moving Image Source*, and *Not Coming to a Theater Near You*. Additionally, he contributed the introduction to Stark House Press' reissue of Clifton Adams' *Death's Sweet Song* and *Whom Gods Destroy*. He also maintains a blog, *Pulp Serenade*. He also plays in the punk band Night Squad (named after David Goodis' novel), and records instrumental music as Modern Silent Cinema.

**Matthew Louis** is a self-taught writer, editor, publisher, graphic artist and jack-of-all-trades. He founded *Out of the Gutter* and *Gutter Books* as a way to deliver the brand of intelligent yet high-impact pulp fiction that he favors but finds rare. Matthew lives in the Pacific Northwest with his family. His most recent book is *The Wrong Man*. To learn about upcoming publications and events visit:

**www.matthewlouis.com**

## Graphic Designer

**Jeff Wong** is a graphic designer and award-winning illustrator who has painted four *Sports Illustrated* covers, most notably their fiftieth Anniversary Issue depicting the entire Sistine Chapel ceiling with sports figures. He has actively collected the work of mystery writer, Ross Macdonald, since first reading the author's work in a detective fiction course in college, and has proudly been a Lou Boxer, NoirCon co-conspirator since 2010. He is currently the Design Director of *Weird Tales* Magazine, which is celebrating its ninetieth anniversary.

**www.jeffwong.com**